Nic

and

The Flight of Argus

15/10/09

Dear Martin
Good luck in Devon
all my love
Liz
x

"Nicodemus is a fairytale that manages to feel both like an ancient legend and a modern mystery play, seamlessly mingling magic and the natural world, creating a timeless and wondrous fantasy world."

—Wildlife TV presenter, Steve Backshall

"A Charming tale with lots for everyone."

—Top ten best selling author, Katie Fforde

"I find the book a delightfully charming story that any child would thoroughly enjoy reading."

—Editor of RSPCA's Animal Action Magazine, Sarah Evans

♣

I am delighted to inform the purchaser of this book, that a percentage of the sales will go to the RSPCA—Enjoy the adventure!

I never saw a wild thing
sorry for itself.
A small bird will drop frozen dead from a bough
without every having felt sorry for itself.

—'Self Pity' by D H Lawrence, 1929

Nicodemus

and

The Flight of Argus

Liz Mente-Bishop

DB

DIADEM BOOKS

Published by Diadem Books

For information, please contact:

Diadem Books
Mews Cottage
The Causeway, Kennoway
Kingdom of Fife
KY8 5JU
Scotland UK

www.diadembooks.com

Cover design and Illustrations by Dr Derek Bishop

ISBN: 978-1-907294-08-2

Printed in Great Britain by the MPG Books Group, Bodmin and King's Lynn

Dedication

To Julia — no matter where in the world you are,
you are always by my side.

Unite with the ones you love
and you can conquer anything!

Acknowledgements

Dr Derek Bishop for his inspiring illustrations.

Charles Muller for his work involved in editing and publishing Nicodemus.

Katie Fforde, for all her precious time, encouraging words and front cover quote.

Steve Backshall for taking time out of his busy schedule for Nicodemus

Sarah Evans for allowing me to 'Go for it!'.

Anna Franklin for her book, 'The illustrated encyclopaedia of fairies'.

Julia, for always being such a great travelling companion and friend.

Mum, for her tireless support and being my audio dictionary!

Dad, for teaching me the good virtues of honesty and commitment.

Tim and Jess for always making me laugh in my hour of need.

Kyra, Dillon and Holly for their boundless energy and enthusiasm.

And Murray for embracing life and everything in it.

Table of Contents

Introduction

Initially I had decided not to do an introduction because when I buy a new book all I want to do is start reading and I thought you might feel the same way. However, it has come to my attention that there are a few things that would be useful for you to know.

So, in no particular order, I wish to point out, my use of:

A) Greek Mythology – I am by no means a connoisseur but in order to write Nicodemus I have done a small amount of research into the amazing world of Greek Mythology. I have been both intrigued and fascinated by what I have discovered and have only touched on the tip of the iceberg, so if Arachne and her spinning or Medussa and her snakes are of interest to you, I would encourage you to do further investigation.

B) Names – Every single character in this book, except Pedros, (who exists) has derived from the meaning of their name; this too was something I thoroughly enjoyed exploring as, let's face it, we all have a name that has a meaning. After the introduction you will find a character list that tells you the meaning of their names. Use this to try and work out what kind of personalities they will have.

C) ‘Big words’ – Some of you reading this will excel in the use of the English language and for those of you, I am truly delighted, because for me growing up with dyslexia, (even in its mildest form) words and reading terrified me. I used to boast, ‘I’ve never read a book’ – but I wasn’t really boasting, I was embarrassed. Unfortunately it has taken me until my thirties to experience the enjoyment that reading and words can give you and I hope in my heart that not a single one of you has to wait that long. So, for those of you with an already comprehensive understanding, I hope that I manage to extend your enormous vocabulary and for those of you, like me, that fear the ‘big word’ I have written a glossary, that you will find at the end of the book. This will not only explain the meaning of the word but will also, in most cases, provide you with an alternative. So the next time you are faced with writing a creative story, you can dazzle your teachers by showing them your new and accurate use of the English language – go on – I dare you!

Enjoy the adventure,

Liz

To find out more information about Liz, Nicodemus and Mykonos visit my website www.nicodemus.uk.com

Characters

In order of appearance

All names are of Greek origin:

Nicodemus: meaning – 'Conqueror for the people'
Pia's husband, Thaddea's father

Ophelia: meaning – 'Wise and immortal'
Nicodemus' Bumble Bee

Acantha: meaning – 'Thorny'
Diomede's mother, Nicodemus' enemy

Zeno: meaning – 'Stranger'
Leader of Acantha's army

Theron: meaning – 'The Hunter'
Zeno's locust

Pia: meaning – 'Heavenly one'
Nicodemus' wife

Thaddea: meaning – 'Courageous being' – A girl of great bravery and endurance.
Nicodemus' and Pia's daughter

Ximena:	meaning – 'Heroine' Nicodemus' niece
Tyrone:	meaning – 'The sovereign' Ximena's Cardinal beetle
Diomede:	meaning – 'Divine ruler' Acantha's son
Ulysses:	meaning – 'The angry one' Diomede's tropical wasp
Stefan:	meaning – 'The crowned one' – A man who wears the victor's laurel wreath Kintfoly king of Delos, Cleopatra's father
Balthasa:	meaning – 'May the lord protect the king' King Stefan's stag beetle
Cleopatra:	meaning – 'Her father's glory' King Stefan's daughter
Lysandra:	meaning – 'The Liberator' Cleopatra''s Tiger moth
Hestia:	meaning – 'A Star' King Stefan's wife
Danae:	meaning – 'Mother of Perseus' Acantha's Hornet
Perseus:	meaning – 'Destroyer' Acantha's hornet, son of Danae

Larissa:	meaning – 'Cheerful maiden' Nicodemus' niece, Ximena's sister
Vanessa:	meaning – 'The butterfly' Larissa's butterfly
Elora:	meaning – 'Light' Thaddea's friend
Cadmus:	meaning – 'Man from the east' – A legendary scholar who devised the Greek alphabet The Newcomer
Aldara:	meaning – 'Winged gift' Cadmus' Emperor dragonfly
Metis:	meaning – 'Wisdom and skill' Golden silk spider
Celosia:	meaning – 'Burning flame' Sylvan fairy
Pedros:	meaning – 'The rock' The pelican
Hermione:	meaning – 'Of the earth' The lizard
Delia:	meaning – 'One who came from Delos' Thaddea's Fire Fly

“What’s the matter? You look like you’ve seen a ghost!”

Chapter 1

The Fall of Beryllos

An unlikely voice, some people may think, but despite his appearance Nicodemus sang like an angel. He used his dulcet tones to lull people gently into a pleasant and restful sleep. It was during one of these relaxing moments that Nicodemus's life was changed forever.

As he lay his head back on his chubby little hands Nicodemus hummed his favourite tune. Alongside him lay his trusted friend and companion Ophelia, who too was a little round, although for a bumble bee that's not such a bad thing. While she slept in the early morning sun a gentle buzz could be heard from her wings, as they quivered tenderly and she lightly toasted her black and golden stripes so they tingled with gratitude. The sky was crystal blue without a cloud to be seen, but if the truth were known, that was the case nearly every morning of the year on the beautiful island of Mykonos.

You may be wondering how Nicodemus' best friend could be a Bumble Bee and I would not be surprised if you are. Nicodemus is a member of The Kintfoly, a race of people who are probably as small as your thumb—but nobody really knows, as they are very hard to find. It is understood they are descendants of The Pitikos—miniature fairies of the Greek Islands. However, unlike The Pitikos, they are not fairies and don't have wings, so as an alternative, have enlisted the help of insects to get around.

"Oh, don't stop now," Ophelia mumbled and twitched her fluffy white tail with frustration, "I was just getting to a good part in my dream."

Ophelia's state of tranquillity was suddenly brought to an abrupt end. Nicodemus scrambled to his feet looking agitated. A few wisps of muddy brown hair had broken free from his ponytail and fallen across his wide eyes and he was tugging at his knotted beard.

"What's the matter? You look like you've seen a ghost!"

Nicodemus did not answer Ophelia's question; instead, the answer was clear by the blackening of the sky and the chill in the air.

"Quick, we must leave at once!" he said. "This has to be the work of that witch Acantha." Breathless with fear, he climbed aboard Ophelia and she took flight with the speed of a shooting arrow.

"What on earth can that evil woman want from us now?" she asked.

"Surely you know what she must be after?"

"We can't let her take the Beryl Stone. Without it our village will be in grave danger." Ophelia's voice sounded desperate.

"It's not the stone I'm worried about." Nicodemus' voice sounded even more desperate.

"We'll get home in time, I promise you; we're nearly…"

"They're not at home," Nicodemus interrupted. "They're in the Sacred Hall planning 'The festival of the crops'."

Ophelia's efforts to reassure him had been in vain. She flew with all her strength but it was not enough to get to the sacred hall before the crazed swarm of locusts. The locusts had surrounded it and were pounding the walls like a giant heart beating.

As they came nearer they could just make out the leader of Acantha's army, Zeno, with his unmistakable black cloak flowing over the back of Theron, known for being the most vicious of all the locusts. Hovering above them was a huge Tropical Wasp and riding it was someone they didn't recognise.

"Who's that?" Ophelia asked.

"I don't know and I'm not sure I want to find out," Nicodemus answered, his heart sinking even deeper with the knowledge that he and his friend could not possibly defeat these dreadful beasts.

By the time they came close enough to see the damage it had inflicted on the hall, the army was departing as quickly as it had arrived. Leaving behind it a mass of devastation and taking with it their precious Beryl Stone, which Nicodemus and Ophelia could just see glinting in the sunlight as it disappeared into the distance.

The Sacred Hall was no longer the thing of beauty that took pride of place over its village but was now a mountain of rubble and dust with its occupants crushed in the fall. Nicodemus jumped off as soon as they landed and ran towards the debris in the hope of finding his family alive and hoping even more so that, for some reason, they had not come to the meeting and were safe at home. Ophelia quickly headed back to the house to check if Pia and Thaddea were there.

In no time at all the villagers began to appear. They were all holding picks, shovels and other tools that could be used to start the rescue efforts.

After finding the house disappointingly empty Ophelia anxiously flew back to where the great hall had once stood. The exterior walls had all been painted white to help reflect the sun on those hot sunny days; the windows and doors were painted a deep sea blue to match that of the perfectly shaped dome that formed the roof, topped only by a simple cross, common of many churches and sacred halls on the island. The inside of the hall had baby blue walls, making it feel nice and cool. Beneath the windows had been delicate tables covered with lace cloths and cut glass bowls filled with petals from the island's most beautiful fuchsia pink 'Bougainvillea' flowers. The sun used to shine through the glass and release great rays of light that shone across the floor in wonderful patterns. The chairs had been hand crafted from wood carved from the fantastic gnarled trees that grew nearby. Standing in the doorway, the overall impression had been truly breathtaking.

Sacred Halls amongst the Kintfoly people were so called because that was where each village housed its most sacred possession: many generations before one of the villagers had found what they later learned to be a human's ring—it was made up of a silver band with a huge blue beryl stone (known to us as an aquamarine). The Beryl stone is believed to bring good luck and give eternal youthfulness to those who own it; also, its qualities are thought to help protect travellers from danger. The villagers chose to keep the ring to see if it would bring them luck.

It had indeed brought them good fortune, as year after year the villagers produced fine crops and they and their insects lived long and healthy lives. To thank the stone for its fortuitous properties they named their village in its honour, calling it 'Beryllos'. Also, every year, the villagers held 'The festival of the crops' during which they had great celebrations. It was while planning for this festival that Nicodemus's wife and daughter found themselves in the Sacred Hall on this fateful day.

Seeing Nicodemus crouched over and shaking hysterically, Ophelia knew something was very wrong.

"Oh Ophelia, we didn't get here in time! How am I ever going to survive without them?" Nicodemus's sobs told Ophelia what she had feared the most, that Pia and Thaddea had been killed when the hall was destroyed.

"Are you sure?"

As Nicodemus rose to his feet, Ophelia's question did not need to be answered. Through the piles of twisted rubble she could see Nicodemus's wife, Pia, lying lifeless, her golden hair covered in dust and strewn across her beautiful face. Next to her was the body of a young girl whose face could not be seen because of the sheer volume of wreckage—but you could make out the bright colours of Thaddea'a best loved jumper. It was the jumper she had been given on her twelfth birthday, and which she had lived in ever since.

Their distress had left them fixed in some sort of trance and the two of them were taken completely by surprise when Nicodemus was knocked to the ground by the wasp and his unidentified rider. His loud cackles could be heard as he spun round and swooped down for a second go. Suddenly a red flash ploughed into him, sending him spiralling out of control.

"That'll teach him, picking on my uncle like that!" Ximena said as she landed. She straightened her jacket and brushed off her broad shoulders, after dismounting 'the red flash', known to her as Tyrone, her cardinal beetle. His hard shell could cause serious damage to anyone who got in his way, especially when he was travelling at speed.

"I haven't finished with you yet, you better watch your back!" came a great yell from the distance.

"Who was that?" Ophelia asked again, only this time to Ximena.

"That, my dear, was Diomede, Acantha's son, with his sidekick Ulysses. Since he turned eighteen Zeno has been training him to be his second in command and he's nothing but trouble, mark my words." Ximena looked around at the desolation, "He'll pay for this, just you wait and see. Has the stone been taken?"

"The stone, Pia, Thaddea, all taken. There's nothing left to live for." Nicodemus's usually jolly face now appeared pale and pained "Come, old friend, I wish to be taken away from this place. It holds nothing sacred for me anymore."

Slowly he pulled himself up onto Ophelia's back. She nodded to Ximena and Tyrone and gently took off. Her grief seemed to be weighing her down, her wings struggling to keep them in the air; but she knew she had to be strong. Nicodemus needed her now more than ever.

Ximena organised some of the other villagers to help sort through the devastation so their friends and relations could be laid to rest in the proper place. As she looked on at the terrible sadness that surrounded her, she swore to avenge the death of her Aunt.

“Father, I will never leave you or the island.”

Chapter 2

Balthasa's Battle

On the neighbouring island of Delos lived King Stefan with Balthasa, his Stag Beetle, his daughter Cleopatra, and Lysandra, her Tiger Moth. The four of them had lived together in Stefan's kingdom since the untimely death of his wife Hestia, during childbirth.

Although they too were Kintfoly they knew nothing of Nicodemus and his village, much in the same way that there are many people in the world who you know nothing about. They spent much of their time exploring the island.

"Father, please tell me something about the island. I love to hear your stories." As they walked together arm in arm Cleopatra pleaded with Stefan.

"All right, my dear. As you know, Delos has no humans living on it and that has been the case since 88BC when the human king of Pontus, Mithridates, waged war against the Roman colony living here and killed all the inhabitants. After that time no one has taken up residence apart from a short period in the 14th century when it became a 'pirates lair'!"

"Well, I'm glad they've gone!"

"I couldn't agree more. Now humans are only allowed to visit the island for a few hours a day so we have plenty of time to look around without the fear of being spotted."

Stefan's kingdom had once been a busy place like the Roman colony but it was not war that had made everyone leave but lack of vegetation, Delos is a barren island, making it very difficult for anyone to survive, be it insects or people (even if they are very small). So gradually the Kintfoly people left the island in search of an easier life and Stefan and Cleopatra were left alone. Although they were not entirely alone, there were still many ants and fire flies and of course lizards, but we don't mention them as they eat the Kintfoly and are more of a threat than the humans!

Whilst Stefan and Cleopatra were enjoying their quiet walk, Stefan felt compelled to ask his daughter something that had been troubling him for some time.

"Darling, are you ever lonely? I worry that now you're a young woman you should be out meeting people of your own age and not at home spending all your days with your ageing father."

As Stefan finished speaking he looked down at Cleopatra. Her auburn hair ran softly down her back and her slight frame appeared fragile, yet she had the inner strength of an entire army. Growing up without a mother had not been easy for her and he only hoped he had done enough to make her happy. It was because he loved her so much that he knew he must let her go.

"Father, I will never leave you or the island. I believe in my heart the right person will come and find me, perhaps when we are least expecting it."

She looked back up at Stefan. He used to seem so grand and formidable, but the last few years had taken their toll. His eyes had sunk back into his face, his skin looked grey and lined and his hair was now completely white. Even his laurel wreath crown looked like it was wilting. At least his long moustache and his thick beard still emphasised his powerful jaw line. Her devotion to him was such that she would never allow him to grow old alone.

Balthasa was back in the kingdom enjoying a relaxing time basking in the sunshine, his ebony shell shining brightly and his eyelids pleasantly warm as they rested over the tops of his beady eyes. As always his ears were on full alert. Protecting the king was a very important job and it was not acceptable to be caught sleeping.

"Balthasa, come quickly. I think we have trouble heading our way!" Lysandra burst into the courtyard flapping her shimmering wings wildly.

Balthasa came round in an instant.

"I'm ready—what have you seen?"

"I hope to God I'm wrong, but I swear I saw Acantha's chariot with those hideous hornets Danae and Perseus." Lysandra was flustered and sheer panic was written all over her face.

"I hope you're wrong, too; she'll be after the kingdom this time for sure. Where did you see them?"

"Heading towards the west wing. Oh Balthasa, what are we going to do?"

"Do you know where Stefan and Cleopatra are?"

"Cleopatra did mention to me they were going to take a stroll to the sheltered garden. It was so hot this morning they wanted to sit in the shade."

"Then I suggest you start there and warn them of Acantha's arrival, and get them to safety."

"And you?"

"I will do my best to hold them off."

"What chance do you have, Balthasa? That's just plain suicide." Lysandra knew she did not have time to argue and, besides, Balthasa's stubbornness meant he would not change his mind anyway.

"I have as good a chance as anyone! My shell is like armour plating—they can't sting me."

Balthasa was right. He certainly stood a better chance than Lysandra. With that she flew off in the direction of the sacred palm.

Balthasa took a deep breath and set off towards the west wing. Sure enough, Lysandra was right and there, in her chariot of thorns, sat the epitome of evil. Her skin was more taut than a stretched canvas: it was extraordinarily pale, almost translucent, which heightened the intensity of her crimson lips. The veins on her neck stood out like claws and her collarbone protruded eerily from her stick-like body. She stared right through Balthasa with her piercing eyes. He froze in mid-air and glanced about feverishly in an effort to see Danae and Perseus. He need not have bothered—they had been expecting him!

Suddenly he was catapulted through the air, hurtling towards the ground at lightening speed. He braced himself for impact. As he crashed to the ground he momentarily lost consciousness, just long enough for Danae and Perseus to have landed either side of him. He shook his head briefly to gather his thoughts and pray for a miracle. He was not going to be taken without a fight, however! Lashing violently with his tremendous antlers he felt one of them tearing the skin of Danae. She let out a shrill scream and stepped back, giving Balthasa the chance to take Perseus one on one. They both had enormous strength and fought ferociously. Neither seemed to be tiring, but thanks to Balthasa's armour and his size overpowering that of Perseus's, he seemed to be gaining the upper hand. Unfortunately, his success was short lived as Danae, recovering from her wound, once again joined the battle. To believe he could take them both would have been foolish.

"Stop, please, just stop! What do you want from us?"

Acantha had joined them and was looking down on him, as he nursed his aching head.

"Want? I don't want anything. I'm having your kingdom. Now step aside while I decide what to do with you."

"You won't find Stefan! He knows you're here and is already building an army to overthrow you." Even though Balthasa knew this was not the case he felt he might unnerve Acantha enough to stop her—wishful thinking on his part!

"You fool, don't insult me with your tales! Your king is building no army—the only thing he should be building is his coffin." Acantha went on: "I have sent Zeno and Diomede to capture him and his spineless daughter and I shall have them chained up by nightfall, and there's nothing you or anyone else can do to stop me." With that she summoned Danae and Perseus to her chariot and left.

"You mustn't worry, you'll be joining your precious king in no time at all, in the dungeons!" Acantha yelled down. "Zeno, take him to join the others."

Balthasa turned to see Theron landing beside him. Zeno, face hidden by his sinister black mask, slid off the side of him and walked round to face Balthasa.

"Thought you could beat her, did you?" Zeno's voice was as deep and mysterious as his appearance.

"You don't scare me! You're just a coward who doesn't even have the courage to show his face." Balthasa stepped forward, holding a proud defensive stance. He may have been captured but he was not going to be submissive for anyone.

"Offend my friend again and you'll face me." Theron thrust his huge circular eyes up close to Balthasa's face.

"Enough now, Theron," Zeno said as he was climbing up onto his back. "We'll finish this another time. Until then, Balthasa, you are to come with me and I shall take you to join Stefan."

They took off over the kingdom walls, passed the sanctuary of Herakles and were heading towards the lion terrace. However, they stopped before they even reached the sacred lake.

"Where are you taking me?"

"You'll find out soon enough." Zeno steered Theron down towards the old well.

Balthasa wondered if he should take this opportunity to escape but dreaded the punishment Stefan might suffer if he did; so instead, he followed Zeno and Theron down to the well.

"This way. Theron, you stay here—I'll be back shortly." Zeno led Balthasa down into the well. It had been many years since there had been any water in it and it was now as dry and dusty as the rest of the island. It got much darker the further down they went and the air became cold and musty. Eventually they came to a large wooden door, with vast iron hinges and bolts. Zeno used his great strength to unlock the door and open it, revealing, to Balthasa's surprise a dungeon purpose built for The Kintfoly.

"Thank God you are safe, old friend. You can't imagine what I've been through, wondering what those reprobates had done to you." Stefan's frail exterior was trembling and his white cloak seemed to engulf him more than ever.

"Likewise, Stefan. Good to see you. Where's Cleopatra and who's this?" Balthasa cast his eyes on a figure huddled in the corner of the room.

"Acantha has taken her to be a slave and has threatened to kill me if she doesn't do what she's told; as for our friend here, I'm afraid I don't know—she hasn't said a word and looks completely terrified. I'm not quite sure how to help her."

Back inside the kingdom walls, Acantha made Diomede knock down the statue of Stefan and replace it with the glowing blue beryl stone. She looked on, running her spidery hands through her wiry black hair; then, when he had finished, she clapped them together in wicked delight.

"Mine, all mine! No one can take it from me now. I shall stay beautiful forever and have everything I want!" Her thin lips curled into a snarl-like grin, just enough to show some of her pointed ivory teeth. Then she turned and strode victoriously back inside to where she had left Cleopatra weeping for her father.

"Oh, do be quiet! It's not so bad. You can think of me as the mother you never had—it'll be fun." Acantha took Cleopatra's delicate chin with one bony fingertip and gently teased it upwards so she could look right into the girl's watery eyes.

"I've never had a daughter. I'm quite looking forward to it."

"Over my dead body!" Cleopatra retaliated.

"As you wish, you foolish child!" Acantha shrieked and raised her hand to strike Cleopatra across the face, but just as she did so Diomede entered the room.

"Excuse me, mother, but I understand from Zeno that Balthasa is now safely locked up with Stefan and our other prize possession and was wondering if there was anything else you wanted me to do."

"Good—and yes, there is. You can take this pathetic thing out of my sight. I don't wish to set eyes on her until she has learnt some respect."

Diomede walked over to Cleopatra and took her arm.

"You'd better show me where your quarters are and then you'll have to stay there until I tell you otherwise." Diomede was firm but could not find it in himself to be unkind to Cleopatra. Together they left the room and continued on, up the spiral staircase to the north tower and finally her bedroom, which had been Cleopatra's special place since she was a little girl and had spent many hours looking out of the window pretending a handsome prince was coming to save her. How she longed for him at this very moment.

As Diomede left she heard a click behind her and realised she was alone, locked in her own sanctuary. She sat down on her mother's favourite armchair, the one that her father and she had sat on many times before. He used to read her bedtime stories while she cuddled up to him and would often fall asleep before he ever got to the end. Glancing out of her window, a single tear ran down her cheek. Hurriedly, she wiped it away.

"I will see my father alive again," she said to herself, "and I shall not shed another tear until I do."

After leaving Cleopatra in the North Tower Diomede chose not to go back to his mother but instead spent some time alone. His pride had been bruised when Ximena had nearly knocked him off Ulysses with that wretched beetle of hers, and he wanted revenge. He decided to get Ulysses and fly back to Mykonos. He would hatch a plan on the way.

"Vanessa, what have they done to you?"

Chapter 3

Used for Bait

Ximena's sister Larissa was landlady of the village Inn. She only had her elegant blue butterfly Vanessa for company and longed for a male companion to grow old with. That was partly why she had opened the Inn—to meet new people. She was very different from her sister, not just in the fact that she did not like to fight and was a quiet person, but also in appearance—Larissa's short, slightly podgy body and bouncy curly brown locks were a stark contrast to Ximena's cropped blonde hair and athletic physique. Nonetheless, the pair of them got on very well and Ximena spent many an hour behind the bar helping her younger sister serve the customers.

Unfortunately, it was a very sombre occasion that had brought them together on this day. They were supplying villagers with refreshments while they fought through the rubble of the sacred hall. It was a long slow process but the good news was that some people had been brought to safety and were recovering with their loved ones. Sadly, the same could not be said for Pia and Thaddea. Their bodies had not yet been recovered and no one other than Ophelia had seen Nicodemus since he had left the site.

"What can we do for Nicodemus?" Larissa asked when they had a quiet moment together. "I feel so helpless."

"I don't know, sis. I think he'll just need time. People say time is the greatest healer." Ximena wasn't convinced herself.

"I want to do more for him. Do you think he'd mind if I took him some food?"

"I'm sure he'd be very grateful, but perhaps not just yet. Maybe you should get Vanessa to ask Ophelia how he's doing."

"I think that's a very good idea. What would I do without you?" Larissa gave Ximena a big hug and felt all the tension being released from her. "I'll find Vanessa now and hopefully have an answer very soon."

"Okay, I'll take these drinks over to the hall and catch up with you later." Ximena gave her sister a quick peck on the cheek and they both went their separate ways.

Before Larissa went out to find Vanessa she thought she would just check on the front bar to see if anyone needed serving.

As she walked through the door she felt her knees weaken and her heart skip a beat, for leaning casually up against the bar was the most attractive man she had ever set eyes on. His skin was bronzed from the sun and his eyes were so dark they were almost as black as his hair, which flopped neatly across his forehead. He looked slightly younger than Larissa and extremely fit and strong.

"Hello there, can I get you something to drink?" she asked, doing her best not to blush.

"That would be lovely, thank you—just some water, please. I've travelled a long way and the sun is blisteringly hot today." His voice was as smooth as melted chocolate and as he finished speaking a very pleasing smile spread across his handsome face.

"It most certainly is—one water coming up!" Larissa felt a little spring of excitement as she poured the man his water.

"So tell me, what on earth happened up on the hill?" he asked. "It looks like a disaster."

Larissa paused for a minute. She hadn't actually stopped to think about what really had happened. It truly was a disaster—her aunt and cousin had been killed with many other villagers. She had been so busy caring for everyone else she hadn't thought of how it would affect her.

"We were attacked by Acantha's army. They stole our precious Beryl Stone, destroyed our sacred hall and killed many of our loved ones." As she said this Larissa felt a huge lump growing in her throat and her eyes filled with tears.

"I'm sorry to hear that," said the man. "Would you like to come outside for some fresh air?" He put his hand out for Larissa to take.

She felt relieved to have the support and warmth of someone to talk to. Together they left the Inn and slowly wandered around to the back garden.

Horror and panic would be the only way to describe what Larissa felt as she came round the corner.

"Vanessa, what have they done to you?" She ran over to her dearest friend who was tied in a net and hanging from the roof of the barn.

"It's all right, Larissa, I'm not hurt." Vanessa's eyes were pricked with fear and her voice was shaking.

"Who did this to you! So help me God they'll regret it." Larissa's voice had changed from shock to anger, her face burning up and beads of sweat appearing on her forehead.

Vanessa didn't answer so Larissa followed her gaze back round to where the man had been standing. He was still there and had now been accompanied by a sleek and brightly coloured tropical wasp, which appeared to be smirking at her.

"Tell me this instant who you are and why you've done this!" Larissa screamed at them.

"I'm Diomede, Acantha's son, and you and your pet are now bait for your sister, who needs to be punished for what she did to me."

Larissa felt so stupid! Ximena was constantly telling her she was too trusting and that she must have her wits about her, and now she had put Vanessa's life at risk as well as her own. This realisation incensed her—and to think she had been attracted to this vile being!

"Whatever she did to you clearly wasn't enough! She won't be held to ransom, trust me. I know her better than anyone and you will regret this. Now, let Vanessa down!" Larissa demanded

"I don't think so, little lady. You and your butterfly are coming on a trip with me and I'm quite sure your sister will rise to the challenge of coming to rescue you. Now you can sit up with me on Ulysses' back if you wish, but if you can't behave I'll have to tie you up with your friend."

"I'm not sitting with you!" Larissa said, outraged by the suggestion.

"You leave me no choice then—give me you hands."

Larissa begrudgingly put out her hands and in no time at all she too had been bundled inside the net with Vanessa. Diomede tied them to Ulysses and quickly ran back inside, scribbled a note to Ximena and left it on the bar. Once back outside he climbed aboard Ulysses and the four of them slowly set off back towards Delos.

On returning to the Inn Ximena found the note. She was absolutely furious and marched straight to Nicodemus's house.

"Nicodemus, quick, open up, I need your help!" she shouted as she banged on the door.

"Go away," was the muffled reply.

"You don't understand, please open the door. They've taken Larissa, and you're the only one who can help me," Ximena begged.

She was relieved to hear the handle turning on the front door. It creaked its way open and there, before her, stood the wreck of her uncle looking torn apart with grief.

"You'd better sit down and tell me what's happened, but I can't see how I can help you." Nicodemus was still in the same clothes he had been wearing when he saw Pia at the hall. He was covered in dust, his bitten fingernails were filled with grime, and his dirty hair had come loose, hanging in his face, making him look very bedraggled.

Realising what a state her uncle was in, Ximena spoke slowly and quietly.

"I'm so sorry about Pia and Thaddea. If there's anything I can do to help, just ask."

"I thought it was my help that was needed," Nicodemus harrumphed.

"Yes, you're right, I do need your help. Diomede has kidnapped Larissa and Vanessa and has challenged me to come and rescue them from the island of Delos."

"I feel for you, honestly I do, but I don't see how I can help you." Nicodemus looked puzzled.

"You're the only one who's ever been to Delos from our village and you are the smartest person I know. Together we'll be able to defeat Acantha and Diomede."

"I'm not interested in going to war with these people. I'm an old man who's lost everything and I don't want to go on anymore." Nicodemus sounded so deflated.

"You're not old and you haven't lost everything. You still have me and Ophelia, not to mention Larissa, whose last words were of you; she was desperate to bring you food and make sure you were okay and this is how you repay her." Ximena realised she had gone too far when…

"How dare you! You've no idea what I've lost and can't possibly imagine what I'm going through. I think it's time you left." Nicodemus was seething when he rose to his feet and flung open the door.

Ximena left with her heart shattered. How could she have been so stupid, speaking to him that way after what he had been through? Larissa was right when she said she only thought about herself. She had behaved so badly and would have to apologise, that is if Nicodemus would ever see her again. She had left herself no choice but to take Tyrone and face Diomede alone. She would leave in the morning.

"Look in the fire, my love."

Chapter 4

The Shadow

Nicodemus was still outraged by the audacity of his niece when he suddenly felt incredibly weak and cold. He realised he hadn't eaten for a long time and at that moment, would have been very grateful for one of Larissa's offerings.

He wondered if he had been too hard on Ximena. She too had suffered the loss of loved ones and on top off that her sister had been taken from her. He decided he would visit her in the morning and make amends, but for now he must get warm and find something to eat.

He lit himself a small fire, for although the days were still warm, as autumn was settling in the nights were getting colder. He and Pia used to enjoy nestling together in front of the fire talking and laughing. A huge sadness swept over him once again; he felt so hollow, as though his heart had been cut from his chest. But he knew he must eat and found some bread and cheese and poured a large whisky to help warm him through.

He sat down by the fire in his old leather armchair. It was nearly as old and worn out as he was. The irony made him smile and he lent back and closed his eyes to enjoy the tingle of the whisky flowing down his throat. He must have dropped off to sleep because the crash of his plate, as it slid off his lap onto the floor, made him jump. He bent down, his knees aching as he did so, and started to pick up the remains of his supper and the shards of the plate.

"Nicodemus, darling, is that you?"

Nicodemus sat back on his heels, alarmed at what he'd heard. He was sure it was Pia's voice. His mouth went dry and he couldn't speak. He thought it must be a dream, so pinched himself hard on his rough cheek.

"It's me Pia, please speak to me."

"Oh darling, is that really you? Where are you?" Nicodemus was searching frantically yet could not see his wife.

"Look in the fire, my love." Her voice was as sweet as it had always been.

Nicodemus crouched back down next to the fire and for a moment could only see the glowing embers in the hearth. Gradually a shape began to form in front of him. It was curling round itself in a tight ball and he could just make out a head. But it was not Pia's; instead, it was in the shape of a snake.

"I don't understand what's happened, am I dreaming?" Nicodemus glanced across at his whisky tumbler and wondered if perhaps he had drunk more than needed to just warm him through.

"No, you're not dreaming, Nicodemus; you're witnessing the greatness of a Stoicheion—you remember 'The Shadow in the Hearth'?

Nicodemus did not answer so Pia's voice continued, "Years ago your father explained to us how a Greek guardian spirit can visit someone, in the form of a snake, appearing to them in the embers of the fire. Well my love, here I am—'Your Shadow in the Hearth'."

Nicodemus's heart filled with joy. To hear his wife's voice again was something he had not deemed possible. When he had seen her lying so still at the hall there had been so much he had wanted to say and now he had the opportunity he was struck dumb.

"Nicodemus, I've been sent to you with great importance. I understand Ximena has asked you to join her on a voyage to Delos to rescue Larissa—is this true?" Pia's voice now sounded urgent.

"Oh my dear wife, I have behaved so thoughtlessly! I threw Ximena from the house, sent her away in her hour of need! How could I have been so selfish!"

"She'll forgive you—she is young and wild but her heart is kind. You must go with her on this journey and take with you these three pieces of advice. Firstly, you must befriend the 'Man from the East'; you will need to be strong for I fear Ophelia will oppose you. Secondly, take the bracelet of iron I made for you; its inner properties may prove indispensable. And finally, the most important of the three, never give in. The journey ahead will be fraught with danger and you may wish to stop the pain and terror and return home. If this happens you must dig deep inside yourself, gather all your courage and go on, I will be watching over you all the way. It is imperative you succeed, as it is not only Larissa who is depending on you but Thaddea too." Pia's voice was becoming faint and the ashes were no longer glowing.

"Thaddea is alive—how? I saw her lying next to you under all the rubble." Nicodemus couldn't believe it; he looked into the fire but it was completely dark now.

"Pia, where are you? Is Thaddea alive? Please tell me or give me a sign."

Pia had gone and Nicodemus was once again alone in his small home on the hill. He was full of hope that his daughter was alive and knew it would be up to him to save her. However, right now there was someone he needed to see and a lot he needed to say, and it could not wait one minute more.

"So why have you been taken prisoner?"

Chapter 5

Torment and Triumph

After their very long and uncomfortable journey Larissa and Vanessa were taken to the dungeon in the well to join Stefan and Balthasa. Once Larissa's eyes had adjusted to the darkness of the cell, she took in her surroundings and introduced herself and Vanessa to the others. Then, from the corner of her eye, she noticed movement from the other side of the room.

"She hasn't said a word," Stefan said. "We don't know who she is or where she's come from, perhaps you could try speaking to her?"

Larissa didn't need to speak to her to find out who she was. She knew as soon as she saw the charming innocence that emanated from the face of her young cousin.

"Thaddea, you're alive! I can't believe it. How, though? We saw you lying next to Pia. Oh, you poor thing, come here and let me hold you." Larissa threw open her arms and wrapped them tightly around Thaddea whose eyes filled with tears. They stood like this for some time before Larissa stepped backwards.

"Thaddea, do you mind if I ask you a question?" Larissa really couldn't understand what had happened. She had definitely seen Thaddea lying next to her mother wearing her favourite jumper.

"No," Thaddea replied meekly.

"If it wasn't you lying next to Pia, who was it and why were they wearing your jumper?"

"It was Elora. We'd been playing a game pretending we lived in each other's houses and had swapped parents. We were having so much fun we even decided to swap clothes. Elora's mother and I had gone outside to gather some fresh petals for the hall, when I was grabbed from behind and whisked off. I could see the building collapsing from the air. I didn't think anyone could have survived, did they?"

"Yes, I think so, I had heard that some people had been rescued, but I was taken before I found out who."

"And mother?" Thaddea questioned tentatively.

"I'm sorry, love." Larissa thought Thaddea was going to start crying again but then she asked the next question.

"Is father all right?" Her face was all red and blotchy, her eyes were puffed out to twice their normal size and her voice was full of concern.

"I'm afraid I don't know. I was just arranging for Vanessa to go and find Ophelia when I was captured." Larissa felt she had let her cousin down by not having word of her father but knew it would have been wrong to lie to her. She looked around for something to sit on and saw some old bits of chewed wood over by Balthasa.

“Sorry, dear I was hungry,” he said shamefully.

“That’s okay, I’ve sat on worse things and it’s better than the cold stone floor.” She smiled at him politely and took one of the logs over to Thaddea who had sat back down by a pile of dry grasses.

Stefan cleared his throat. “Excuse me, dear, I’m sorry if it’s rude to ask, but do you know what’s going on and why we’ve all been imprisoned?”

“I’ll do my best,” Larissa began. “This is Thaddea, my cousin, and her father Nicodemus, has crossed paths with Acantha before and not in a good way! He banished her from our village many years ago for being wicked and unkind to the other villagers. Acantha was told never to return and she warned Nicodemus she would seek her revenge. From what I can make out she’s stolen our beryl stone, under the assumption it will bring her good fortune and eternal youthfulness. Then, in order to hurt Nicodemus the most, she had his wife Pia killed and his daughter kidnapped. And if that wasn’t enough, now she’s taken over your kingdom.”

“So why have you been taken prisoner?” Stefan was still trying to piece the puzzle together.

“I’m not exactly sure, but Diomede told me that my sister, Ximena, needed to be punished for what she’d done to him and I was to be used as bait to lure her into a trap.”

“What did she do?”

“If I know my sister, she gave as good as she got but whatever it was, it’s certainly made Diomede mad.”

“I see,” Stefan nodded. “Do you think your sister will come?”

"I don't doubt for one moment she'll come. I just hope she can get to Diomede before he gets to her."

Before they could continue their conversation the door opened and Diomede entered.

"Someone wishes to see you," Diomede said pointing at Larissa.

Thaddea grabbed hold of her cousin's arm, desperate for her to stay.

"It's okay, don't worry, I won't be long and the others will look after you."

"Promise you'll come back, Larissa! I can't stand the thought of losing you too."

"I promise." Larissa kissed Thaddea gently on the forehead and walked towards the door.

"And just so you don't try anything stupid, like escaping, we'll be taking Vanessa too," Diomede added.

The pair of them were escorted out and taken back to the kingdom.

"We'll take her from here." Danae said once they were inside, her villainous eyes glinting with intent and her antennae flicking in a sinister manner. She was enjoying this—they hadn't had a victim for a long time and this pathetic specimen would be fun to torment.

Vanessa looked across at Larissa. The fear was back in her eyes, although even deeper than before, and her beautiful electric blue wings were fading as though the colour was being drained by every word spoken. Larissa felt defenceless; her dearest friend was to be subject to unknown atrocities at the hands of these brutes and she was powerless to stop them. Sadly, she watched as they took her away.

"I'll do whatever you want, but please don't let them hurt Vanessa. You must know the things your mother has made you do are wrong. How can you behave this way?" Larissa persisted, appealing to Diomede's better nature. "I feel sorry for you. In my opinion a life with no love is not worth living. I myself would rather be dead than feel alone." She could not help herself, for she always believed there was good in everyone and was certain that Diomede was just suffering under the hands of his mother.

"I don't need your pity!" he retorted. "Now follow me."

As they walked along the corridors Larissa admired the splendour of the building; the high patterned ceilings, which had coloured slightly with age, and the wooden panelled walls that creaked as if they were speaking to her. There was a distinct smell in the air although she couldn't quite place it and decided it was just that of the kingdom itself.

Eventually they came to a long narrow hall that seemed to stretch further than the eye could see. As they entered, the temperature dropped dramatically. Larissa felt the hair on the back of her neck stand tall, like soldiers on parade. Her feet embedded themselves into the battered and threadbare rug that lay beneath them. Her breathing quickened and her hands became clammy. She was suddenly startled when a bitter voice came from the distance.

"Come closer, I wish to see this so-called great warrior that took it upon herself to knock my son off his ride, obviously failing as only a little wretch like you could possibly achieve."

As Larissa walked closer to the voice, she realised it was coming from behind a large black screen, embossed with gold Japanese figures, fitting for the surroundings, she thought briefly. She carefully came around the side giving it a wide berth.

"Is this it? Why am I surprised, Diomede, you are as useless as this creature before me! She is no warrior. She is not capable of doing her hair let alone doing any damage to my existence. The only one likely to do that is you, by proving that you are completely unworthy of being called my son."

Acantha spoke with such venom that Larissa really did feel sorry for Diomede, even though what he had done was unforgivable. No one deserved to be so cruelly treated, especially by their own mother.

"But mother, you don't understand…"

"The only thing I don't understand is how I've tolerated you for so many years! Now get out!"

It was plain to Larissa that Diomede had lost the desire to explain the situation and, as he turned to leave, she could see his hard exterior had been reduced to nothing more than that of a schoolboy who had just been reprimanded by his headmaster in front of all his friends. Strangely, she felt she must defend him.

"Acantha, I presume," she began

"Oh, so you're not as stupid as you look then?"

"You may bully your son but you won't bully me," she gulped hard before continuing, "I'm not the person who ran into Diomede, although I wish I were; it was in fact Ximena, who is a great warrior and you'd better watch out because she's on her way. Despite what you may think of your son, he'd devised a cunning plan to lure her away from the safety of our village in order that she may rescue, as you so pleasantly put it, her useless sister. Namely, me."

"You may not be a warrior but you've been gifted with an unnecessary amount of insolence! If I were in your shoes I don't think I would be so sure of myself. Besides, look out of the window—I have something to show you." Acantha stepped back and airily waved her skeletal hand in the direction of the courtyard.

As Larissa headed towards the window she was sure she had never seen one so enormous in her life. It was taller than she was and didn't look as if it had been touched for many years. As she got closer she could feel the warm breeze seeping in through the old wooden frame. It was a nice feeling and for a fleeting moment she was back in the garden of her Inn with Ximena sipping a nice cold beer.

Her daydream was brought to a halt when below her she saw Vanessa hanging from some contraption she could only imagine was used for torture. It had high wooden posts with cables hanging down; connected to these were large iron clamps, and attached to those, to Larissa's horror, were Vanessa's wings. Seeing her friend like that enraged Larissa. She swung round.

"You scoundrel! What do you want?" She wished she could use her size to squash Acantha until she drew her final breath, but she knew that would only mean the death of her friend, so she had to stay calm.

"I don't think I've ever been called a scoundrel before—I quite like it," Acantha smirked. "You have a choice—you will activate the Beryl Stone or I will have your friend tortured." She was very pleased with herself and sat down on an elegant high backed armchair that had burgundy velvet upholstery, knotted brass arms and tapered legs. She felt really rather regal. Well, she did have her own kingdom now! Perhaps she should call herself Queen Acantha. The thought made her smile with satisfaction. She did not need her hopeless son—she and Zeno could conquer everything. Once Diomede had done all her dirty work she would dispose of him.

"No one can activate the Beryl Stone. Its powers are held within, and how they are released is unknown. This is not something you can dictate, Acantha—not even you can tell it what to do. I should imagine it has chosen not to charm you with eternal youthfulness as you simply don't deserve it, and as for good fortune, didn't you know that one good turn deserves another and as that is something you have never accomplished, I think you're going to have a long wait." Larissa was secretly delighted that the stone had refused to show its powers in Acantha's presence. However, that was not going to change the fact that she would be furious and someone would have to pay. Larissa's heart was stabbed by her thoughts of Vanessa.

"Perhaps you are as stupid as you look." Acantha's eyes were wild like fire. "I don't make idle threats, you imbecile!" She lent on the window and screamed: "Do your worst!"

"Nooooo!" Larissa yelled in vain. She turned and ran along the hall, tears streaming down her cheeks, shouting 'No' over and over again until her voice was hoarse.

Down in the courtyard Danae heard the words that were like music to her ears. She and Perseus took turns to poke and taunt Vanessa. They tore at her wings and with a terminal stroke Danae thrust her sting into Vanessa to release the venom.

"Quickly, Acantha wants you! She wishes to be taken to the sacred lake immediately," Cleopatra improvised as she ran round the corner and shouted to Danae and Perseus.

This startled Danae just enough to make her pull her sting from Vanessa before all of the venom could be injected. Then she and Perseus flew off in search of Acantha.

As they disappeared Cleopatra knew she did not have much time until they realised it had been a trick. Fortunately Lysandra flew to her assistance and together they worked to set Vanessa free. Lysandra flapped her wings, desperately trying to keep Vanessa's weight off the cables, while Cleopatra struggled to release the clamps. Eventually, after what seemed like a lifetime, Vanessa was free.

"Can you fly?" Cleopatra asked

"You just try and stop me! I'm going to find Nicodemus and get help. Tell Larissa I love her." And with that Vanessa set off with the determination of a bull after a red rag.

Arriving in time to see her friend escape was too much for Larissa and she fell to her knees, her whole body shaking, incapable of stopping the tears—only now the tears of sadness had been joined by tears of joy.

"Thank you both," was all she could muster. Cleopatra took hold of her and held her tight, Lysandra stayed close to keep watch.

"Nice to see you have a soft side."

Chapter 6

Time to Make the Peace

This had to have been the longest and most painful day of Nicodemus's life. It had started with being woken bright and early by the floating coral pink haze of sunlight coming in through his miniature windows. He had looked across at his loving wife and noticed her cheeks glowing from the warmth of the sun. Gently he had stroked her soft hair and fondly squeezed her hand before he kissed her goodbye, for the last time. He had arranged with Ophelia to go for an early morning fly; they agreed it was the best time to go, before the sun got too hot. They would find somewhere comfy and quiet to relax, sing and enjoy each other's company, commonly known as their favourite pastime.

What a tragic end to such a beautiful beginning, his darling wife so tender and pure having been taken from him forever and their plans for the future demolished along with that of the sacred hall. His Niece, Larissa, kidnapped by his archenemy and just when she needed his help the most Nicodemus had sent Ximena away.

As the long day was drawing to a close Nicodemus did at least have one glimmer of hope to spur him on. Although he could not be certain he was pretty sure that Thaddea was alive and it was this news that had led him to call for Ophelia and warn her of their impending journey.

"Ophelia, you're my dearest friend and what I'm asking of you is no small request. This journey will be extremely dangerous and I have no guarantees we'll survive. Are you ready?"

"When do we leave?" Ophelia smiled in a bee kind of way and was relieved to see Nicodemus regaining his spirit. "And what do you need me to do?" she added.

"Firstly, we need to find the saddle and pouches and then organise all the equipment. This will be quite an ordeal for an old pair like us."

"Speak for yourself, old man, but I'm fit as a fiddle, or perhaps that should be as fat as a fiddle!" Together they both let out a great belly laugh. It was good to release some pressure; they knew they had to get through this somehow and laughing was a good way to start!

Regaining his composure, Nicodemus continued, "We'll also need food and water. I can't think straight when I'm hungry. Oh, and I must remember the bracelet from Pia."

"What was it like?"

"It's quite plain, apart from the catch which contains minute pieces of shell that glitter like diamonds."

"No sorry, I meant, what was it like talking to Pia?" Ophelia looked away as she asked this question, worried that it might bring Nicodemus's brighter demeanour down again but she had been amazed that the legend of the Stochieon was true and wanted to hear more about it.

"Oh I see. It was wonderful just to hear her voice once more. I treasured every second. It was literally as the legend describes, a snake curled up in the hearth talking to me—truly amazing." Nicodemus trailed off, temporarily revisiting the moment. "Anyway, back to work, it's late; we've a big adventure ahead of us and it's time for me to make my peace with Ximena."

Nicodemus quickly cleaned himself up and changed his clothes; then he and Ophelia gathered what they needed and set off to find Ximena. Although it was night, the sky was not dark; instead, it was shadowed by a tremendous ivory glow from the stars twinkling in the bright moonlit sky. They were quiet on the short journey to Ximena's, both mentally preparing for what might lie ahead.

It was very late by the time they arrived and Nicodemus did wonder if it would be rude to wake her. He decided it was too important to wait and took the plunge, banging loudly on the door.

"Okay, okay, I'm coming," came an agitated voice from the inside. Ximena opened the door, her usual military-style clothing replaced with floral pyjamas.

"Nice to see you have a soft side." Nicodemus said, trying to break the ice.

"Don't you dare tell anyone or I'll break your nose!" Ximena responded flatly, glaring straight into Nicodemus's kind blue eyes.

This made him shift nervously from one foot to the other and then he noticed Ximena's harsh exterior soften and gradually a smile began to creep across her stunning face. He had never really noticed how striking she was, but seeing her without her normal fighting bravado, he realised she had lovely rose coloured lips, great sculptured cheekbones sweeping upwards to her hypnotic green eyes—quite a picture, he thought. Without needing to speak he knew he had been forgiven, so he let out a long sigh of relief and spread open his welcoming arms into which Ximena gladly stepped, resting her head on his vast chest while he folded his arms lovingly around her. She didn't mind him seeing her like this; it wasn't easy being tough all the time and sometimes a hug is just what you need—don't you agree?

Ximena invited Nicodemus to come in and get some sleep. They would set off in the morning when they were all feeling refreshed.

“They could have got us all killed.”

Chapter 7

The Newcomers

Nicodemus woke early with his head thumping, the turmoil of the previous day obviously showing. He got himself up and dressed and was just leaving when he caught sight of himself in the mirror. His beard was even more knotted than normal, so he spent a moment splitting it into sections and twirling it. It looked a bit like dreadlocks but that didn't matter; at least it was a bit tidier. One last look in the mirror and he flared his rounded nostrils. This had always made Pia laugh and it was just enough to make him smile. He closed the door behind him and went downstairs.

Ximena was already up and back into more suitable attire; khaki trousers with more pockets than a submarine full of cadets, black boots that laced up nearly to her knees, a moss green long sleeve top with padded elbows and shoulders and a camouflage waistcoat with beret to match. Nicodemus looked down at his clothes—nut brown trousers with a hole in the knee and a cream coloured shirt with three buttons missing, Pia had been a wonderful wife but sewing was not her strong point. He simply raised one thick bushy eyebrow and took a seat at the table next to a pot of steaming hot coffee.

"Set you up for the day good and proper, Unc," Ximena said cheerily, sitting down next to him and pouring them both a cup.

"I do wish you wouldn't call me that, Ximena—it sounds so…"

"Young and cool? Yes, I know, but you wouldn't understand at your age, would you?" She laughed and jumped back up to get some bread for them both.

When they had finished eating they went to find Ophelia and Tyrone who, after having found themselves a suitable breakfast of sweet nectar from Ximena's petite but well kept garden, were seated discussing the best way to Delos. As they spoke, Tyrone cleaned his ferocious looking toothed antennae and Ophelia was relieved to be his friend; she didn't fancy the chances of any opponent that might come up against him. She did find it ironic, though, that both he and Ximena had such fierce outward appearances yet were soft as putty when it came to flowers—a good job Acantha was not aware of their 'Achilles heel', she thought.

"Time to make a move, everyone," Nicodemus announced once they were all together. He carefully attached Ophelia's saddle. He wouldn't normally use it because it was very uncomfortable for her but they didn't have much choice—they were going to be doing a lot of flying and without it she would become extremely sore; also, they depended on all the pouches to hold their equipment.

"Sorry about this, Phe, I know you don't like it."

"It's okay, some things are just more important."

"I'm so glad I have you. Don't you ever leave me!"

"As I'm sure you already know, Ophelia means immortal, so I'm not planning on going anywhere!" Ophelia told him proudly.

"That's all very well, but my name means 'conqueror for the people', so I wouldn't be so sure if I were you!"

"Patience, my friend, you'll see," Ophelia said and then waited quietly while Nicodemus organised himself.

Presently he addressed the others: "Would you all agree with me if I suggested the best way to get to Delos would to be to leave from Chora on one of the human boats that take the tourists?"

"Why can't we just fly? I'm strong enough." Tyrone seemed put out.

"I know you are; however, what we have to remember is that Diomede and Acantha's army will be waiting for us on the other side and we have no idea where they'll be or where they've hidden Thaddea and Larissa, so I think we should conserve our energy as much as possible, so when we arrive, we are ready to fight, if we need to."

Tyrone seemed content with this explanation, as did the others, and together they took off and headed west towards Chora.

It was still relatively early and they were leaving behind them a stunning sunrise filled with gorgeous soft pinks and warm shades of orange. It was better for them, though, as they were flying away from the sun, which made visibility easier. Only the hum of wings could be heard from the four of them, each using the time to reflect on the events from the day before and anticipate what might be lying in wait for them.

They had only been in the air for a short time when they heard a loud yelling and buzzing sound hurling towards them from behind. They slowed down and turned round in an effort to work out what was causing all the commotion. A silhouette against the pretty skyline appeared to be heading for them like a meteor from outer space. Dumbfounded, the four of them just hovered, staring at it in disbelieve. The dark shape was spinning violently with arms, legs and wings flailing in all directions; from it came piercing shrieks and uncontrollable laughter, making it difficult to decipher if the imminent visitors were in trouble or just out having lots of fun.

They had all been so mesmerised by the object before them, that none of them had thought to get out of the way. Then all of a sudden it was so close they didn't have time and with an almighty thud it bulldozed straight into them. There was utter pandemonium, people clinging on for dear life swirling around, upside down and down side up. Nicodemus imagined this was what it felt like for the humans on their big merry-go-rounds and didn't fancy the idea in the least. Ximena managed to gain control first and had actually quite enjoyed herself.

"Wow, that was incredible!" she exclaimed. "Who are you guys, and what on earth were you doing? You should have been more careful—you could have got us all killed."

"Quite right, they could have got us all killed—totally irresponsible!" Ophelia was highly unimpressed and if she could have crossed her arms and tutted, believe me she would have.

"Okay everybody, let's calm down," Nicodemus said, using his best skills of diplomacy. "Hello, I'm Nicodemus and this is Ophelia." He could feel her fur bristling beneath him and could sense she did not approve of the newcomers. Nonetheless, he persevered: "Would you two be so kind as to give us your names and explain exactly what you were doing!"

The new arrivals looked a bit sheepish and it was the rider who spoke. "Nice to meet you. I'm Cadmus, named after the legendary scholar who devised the Greek alphabet." He seemed to swell in confidence with every word. "And this is my ultimate masterpiece in aerodynamics—Aldara." He gestured proudly towards the most magnificent emperor dragonfly the group had ever seen; her tail was an intensifying and shimmering sapphire blue blending naturally into a flawless turquoise abdomen and topped with a glimmering celadon face that was streaked with silver. She seemed to blush slightly, having been given such a grand introduction.

Cadmus went on: "We're sorry about running into you, but we recently discovered Aldara could fly upside down and we wanted to know what it felt like."

"Looks to me like you need more practise. I'm Ximena, by the way, and this is Tyrone." She smiled, observing the young man before her. He wore jet black, thick rimmed glasses with such a strong magnification that his eyes bulged from his face like a frog. He was a bit on the scrawny side and wore navy blue and blood red chequered trousers with brown leather brogues and a crisp white shirt, buttoned all the way up to his chin, definitely an academic and not very streetwise, she surmised, although he seemed nice enough.

Ophelia on the other hand was completely underwhelmed by the whole affair and had found herself feeling quite uppity. "We're on a very important mission and don't have time for people like you slowing us down, so if you would kindly be on your way we can carry on our business, without any further delay."

"I really am sorry about what happened. If there's anything we can do to make up for it, we'd be only too glad." Cadmus got the impression Ophelia was not going to be easily swayed.

"I don't think so, thank you. Now if you would please…"

"Actually," Nicodemus butted in, "I think we need all the help we can get, so I would be very grateful if you would join us on our journey." It was a good job he couldn't see the daggers that Ophelia's eyes were throwing at him. "However, you will need to behave and no silly cavorting is allowed."

"That's very kind of you, Nicodemus; what exactly are we letting ourselves in for?"

"I could ask the very same question," Ophelia grumbled.

"Perhaps you could fill Cadmus and Aldara in on what's happened," Nicodemus asked Ximena, "while Ophelia and I have a quick word."

"Is she always like that?" Cadmus asked when the others were out of sight.

"She can be a bit like a house matron at times, but she only has our best interests at heart and by the time I've explained everything I think you'll understand."

Meanwhile, finding they were far enough away from earshot, Ophelia demanded to know what Nicodemus was up to. "Are you insane, letting those two reckless youngsters join us? It was going to be hard enough without having to babysit them as well."

"I'm sorry, Ophelia, but I promised Pia I would befriend 'The man from the East'."

"What makes you so sure this is him?"

"Not only did he arrive from the direction of the sunrise, but his name, Cadmus, actually means 'Man from the East'. You must see, Phe, this has to be him." Nicodemus was convinced this was the right thing to do and despite what Ophelia said and did, he was determined to stick to his decision.

"I'm only doing this because we've been friends for so long and Pia must have had a genuine reason to ask you. I'm warning you, though, if there's any nonsense, I'm off. I'm not putting our lives in danger, particularly when we have Thaddea to think of."

All things considered, Nicodemus was quite relieved by her response.

…clawing his face to relieve her anger.

Chapter 8

Acantha's Scorn

Vanessa's escape had sent Acantha into a psychopathic frenzy, much like that of a rabid dog. She had screamed at Diomede so loudly they were lucky the building hadn't collapsed around them. After humiliating him (one time too many) and clawing his face to relieve her anger, she finally discharged him under the premise that he could not return until he had found and destroyed Vanessa once and for all.

As he and Ulysses left into the dusk, Cleopatra and Larissa looked on in bewilderment. Never had either one of them witnessed anything like it before.

"This is so awful! How can I feel sorry for that man, when, not only was he responsible for, my kidnapping, but he's now on the way to hunt Vanessa down, like some wild animal and, kill her." Larissa was feeling very emotional and confused.

"Don't be so hard on yourself. I think anyone would have felt sorry for him if they'd heard what she'd said. Fancy having a mother like that! Are you going to be okay?"

"I'll be fine, thanks, and I'm sure you're right—things are just a bit strange at the moment. I'm Larissa, by the way." She put her hand out for Cleopatra to shake.

"Cleopatra—nice to meet you."

"How are you caught up in all this?"

"This kingdom belongs to my father, Stefan. He was captured and locked up somewhere. Lysandra and I are being held as slaves for Acantha and I had just escaped from my room, when I heard all the screaming and knew I had to come and help.

"Sorry, did you say your father was Stefan?"

"Yes, why? Do you know him?"

"I don't know him exactly, but he's being held with Balthasa and Thaddea in a dungeon hidden in this huge well. I'd only been there for a little while when I was summoned by Acantha.

"Is he okay?"

"He was okay when I left, or at least as okay as you can be in these circumstances."

"Thank goodness for that." Cleopatra was just about to ask who Thaddea was when she realised Lysandra was missing. She instantly started to panic, knowing full well that Acantha would not rest until someone had paid for Vanessa's escape. "Lysandra's gone, quick, we must go back and find her!"

They retraced their steps; they had been on their way back to the North Tower when the commotion between Acantha and Diomede had caused them to stop in their tracks. It had seemed only moments before that they had been faced with Vanessa hanging in the torture trap, but now it was Lysandra's turn—in just the same way, clamped by her wings, looking weak and defenceless. Only this time it was not the hornets inflicting the pain but Zeno and his locusts.

Before the pair of them had any chance of concocting some kind of rescue plan they were grabbed from behind by two of Zeno's locusts. Larissa was taken back to the dungeon to join Stefan and the others while Cleopatra was brought before Acantha.

"In case you hadn't noticed, I'm not having a good day!" she spat the words out, forcing Cleopatra's head to involuntarily shoot backwards, "and someone is going to have to pay. Until I get news that Diomede has disposed of that irritating butterfly I shall leave your darling moth hanging there for all to see. Just a precautionary measure, you understand—a little reminder of who's in charge around here."

"How long do you think you can keep this up, Acantha? No one is invincible and when father escapes you'll see that."

"I think that's unlikely; even if your ancient father manages to free himself from the dungeon he'll find it surrounded by snakes, which will devour him in an instant, leaving not so much as a trace of his existence."

"Well, Nicodemus then," Cleopatra was refusing to allow Acantha to believe her current position was unthreatened, although she wasn't even sure who Nicodemus was; she just remembered Vanessa saying she was going to find him.

"That great lump, I don't know how that bossy bee of his ever gets off the ground! He's as round as he is high and is certainly no match for me; besides, I've sent him a beautiful gift that will soon put a stop to his heroic efforts to rescue his daughter."

'I wonder if Thaddea is his daughter?' Cleopatra thought to herself before asking, "What beautiful gift?"

"Never you mind, but rest assured even if Nicodemus fails to succumb to the lure of the Sylvans, the Dactyls protecting the Beryl Stone, will definitely finish him off."

Cleopatra had no idea what Acantha was talking about. What were Sylvans and Dactyls, and how on earth was she going to get out of this mess. She hoped Nicodemus, whoever he was, would arrive soon and put an end to this terrible nightmare.

Cadmus was clinging on for dear life.

Chapter 9

Appearances can be Deceiving

Having now established that four was to become six, Nicodemus and the others had flown to a secluded spot, away from any humans, to reassess their plans and check their stocks. Ophelia became even more livid when they discovered that they had lost all their supplies during the escapades of that morning. Fresh water is very scarce on Mykonos and this meant they would need to venture into the world of the humans to fill their canisters.

It was decided that as Cadmus and Aldara had been the primary cause of their predicament, they would be the ones to undertake the mission. Nicodemus also believed it would be a good way for them to show Ophelia how responsible they could be—an error on his part, it has be said!

Ximena and Nicodemus, in the meantime, decided to find some food. Ophelia was still in a temper so Nicodemus went on foot. This proved to be completely exhausting and with very little reward. The terrain was not like his little village that was purpose built for his size, and Nicodemus found he was walking for hours and not really getting anywhere. He was becoming very hot and cross and had decided to go back and force Ophelia to fly him somewhere, when he got a sudden waft of food in the breeze. Briskly he headed towards the smell. He couldn't see anything in front of him and was so busy looking round that he nearly fell head first into a huge chasm. It would not have been huge to us, of course; in fact, it was merely a drain hole with a slatted cover, but to Nicodemus it was like the Grand Canyon. As he stood teetering on the edge of it, he caught sight of the item producing that lovely smell. His stomach gave a timely rumble and he carefully crawled down, having looped his rope round him and one of the slats. When he reached the food he was pleased to see it was the leftovers of someone's burger and he started to tuck in. It was stone cold and to us a completely disgusting proposition, but for Nicodemus it was total heaven. He ate until he couldn't take another bite; slowly he pulled himself up to the roadside and headed back to where he had left Ophelia.

In the meantime Cadmus and Aldara set off in search of some bottled water. They found themselves in a small village with a few shops and restaurants. They just needed to decide where to stop and how they were going to fill up without being noticed. They hovered over a pretty looking establishment that had a selection of wicker tables and chairs set up outside; each table had beautiful flowers for a centrepiece and they could see lots of humans laughing and having fun.

"This is the place," Cadmus announced.

"Okay, where shall I land?"

"Let's go around the back. There's bound to be somewhere you can wait while I go in."

"As you wish, boss!" Aldara said with a mischievous smile.

"Very funny, young lady, you do realise we need to get this right; we're in enough trouble as it is." Cadmus was taking this very seriously. They flew around the corner and Aldara set herself down on a window ledge, being careful to make sure she couldn't be seen.

Cadmus dismounted and lowered himself down onto the shiny stainless steel worktops. This wasn't going to be easy. There were humans everywhere and, more to the point, there were humans everywhere holding big knives. He took a deep breath and tiptoed between the utensils, skipped over the plates and scurried between the pots. Eventually he arrived at the service area where all the bottles were lined up. Suddenly an enormous hand lurched towards him. He froze solid like an ice pop but fortunately it was heading for one of the bottles of water next to him. Cadmus vigorously wiped away the sweat from his forehead, glanced around wildly and started to climb up the side of one of the bottles. Once he reached the top he was mortified to discover he couldn't open the lid. What was he going to do now? He couldn't go back empty handed. Apart from the fact that Ophelia would never forgive him, he would be letting Nicodemus down and he had trusted him to get this right. Frantically, he searched for more water. He was delighted when he saw some tiny glasses—tiny for humans, that is, all lined up on a waiter's trolley, full to the brim and ready to be served.

Courageously he ran for it, ducking and diving out of danger with an amazing amount of precision. Gratifyingly, he arrived at the trolley unscathed, trying to control his breathing and not pass out. He walked over to one of the glasses. His adventure had left him so thirsty that, perching precariously on the edge of the glass, he filled up his canister and gulped it down in one go. He let out a rasping cough and shook his head. That was strong water, he thought, though lovely and sweet! He was still thirsty and promptly drank another one, this time without the cough, so he assumed it was just because he had drunk the first one too quickly. Just as he was filling up his canister for the third time he began to feel slightly strange, a bit wobbly and light-headed. Before he knew it he had fallen head first into the glass! He started to thrash about spluttering and swallowing more fluids, then relaxed enough to realise that he could just reach the edge of the glass; so with a tremendous heave he pulled himself up and toppled, with a wet slap, onto the trolley.

As he got to his soggy feet he saw his canister lying next to him. He picked it up to find it was already quite full. It must have filled up while he was inside the glass, he thought.

The journey back to Aldara was an interesting one. For some reason things had started to appear blurry and he was seeing double. This was very disconcerting as he had found it difficult to avoid the humans in the first place, let alone now when he couldn't see straight. It was not just his vision that was all wonky—walking was proving a problem as well. The simple task of putting one foot in front of the other was completely beyond Cadmus' capabilities and the whole situation was gradually turning into one great big joke.

Suddenly Cadmus was taken over by a fit of uncontrollable giggles. He knew this was a bad idea and someone was bound to notice him, but he couldn't stop himself! He tried slapping his face, but this only made matters worse as he thought it was hilarious and only laughed harder. His amusement was brought dramatically to an end when a giant hairy hand slammed down on the top of the work surface, which sent plates and Cadmus flying across the kitchen. Although startled, Cadmus was greatly relieved as he had ended up right under the windowsill where Aldara was waiting. There was total chaos in the kitchen with humans yelling at each other and running about all over the place.

"*Psst, Psst.* Aldara, can you hear me? Quick, I need your help. You have to come and get me."

"Where are you?"

"Down here, dummy, where d'you think." Cadmus was becoming very anxious now.

"There's no need to be rude, especially as I'm rescuing you!" Aldara snapped as she swooped down, picked up Cadmus, flew back out of the window and landed in a nearby tree.

She put Cadmus down rather roughly because she was cross with him for speaking to her that way.

"Ow, there's no need to be like that." He said trying to get to his feet but staggering all over the place.

"Well, I think there is and is there something you'd like to say to me?"

"Er, yes, I think so. Actually, I'm not sure—what do I need to say?"

"How about thank you! What's the matter with you, Cadmus—you're acting really weird."

"I don't know—I feel pretty weird, I must say. Oh. I did get some water though—do you want some?"

"I wouldn't mind. Perhaps you could tip some into my mouth?"

Cadmus held up the canister and gave her what he thought was water. Instantly she knew what was wrong with Cadmus, but instead of telling him she decided she would have some fun.

"That's lovely and refreshing. I think you ought to have some more as you're looking very hot and flustered."

"Yes, I think I will. We better not have too much, though, or there won't be any left for the others."

"Go on, drink up—it'll be alright. We can always get more later." Aldara didn't really want any to be left for the others, not now she knew what it was, that was for sure.

"*Hic*, I think we should—*hic*—go now. *Hic*, stand still so I—*hic*—can get on." Not only was Cadmus struggling to stand up straight but now he also had the hiccups.

"I *am* standing still," Aldara replied with a crafty smile. "Here," she said as she lowered her head. "Perhaps you should climb up this way."

Cadmus clambered up in the most ungainly fashion and, once on Aldara's back, sat upright to find he was facing backwards. Sensing his plight, Aldara swiftly took off before he had a chance to turn round.

"*Woa*, Aldara—*hic*. I'm not ready, I'm going to fall off. Slow—*hic*—down! I need to turn round." Cadmus was clinging on for dear life.

"Trust me, this is the perfect way to get rid of hiccups," Aldara said just as she did a huge loop and then continued by flying backwards. "Is that better? You can see where you're going now."

"Oh God, I think I'm going to be sick," Cadmus said with his hands over his mouth.

"You'll be alright and the good news is, it sounds like your hiccups have gone." Although Aldara thought this was highly amusing she slowed down and steadily turned round; besides, no amount of fun is worth someone being sick on you—I'm sure you feel the same way.

"Why don't you spin round? We're nearly back now."

"My head's already spinning. I'm not sure I can handle any more," came the mumbled reply.

Just in the nick of time Aldara saw the rendezvous point. She landed gracefully just inside the entrance to a small cave, sitting snugly in the long stone wall that ran parallel to the beach. Cadmus slid off the side and collapsed in a sopping wet heap looking like something the cat had dragged in—then without any warning vomited all over the floor.

"Will someone kindly explain to me what on earth is going on here?" Ophelia bellowed.

"Cadmus got some water," Aldara giggled.

Ophelia decided she had no intention of dealing with this charade and left Nicodemus to sort it out.

He picked up Cadmus's canister and took a small sip. As calmly as he could he tipped the remaining contents away down a crack in a stone.

"What did you do that for—I nearly died getting that water!" Cadmus said while he clutched his head as a result of the sheer volume of his own voice.

"That, my dear boy, was not water, it was in fact Ouzo, a strong liquor drunk by humans and me from time to time, but certainly not designed to be drunk in the vast quantities I can only imagine you've just consumed."

"Oh no, I thought it tasted a bit sweet." Cadmus groaned. "I think I'm going to be sick again." Poor Cadmus writhed as his stomach rejected yet more of the dreaded Ouzo.

Nicodemus turned to Aldara. "You knew about this, didn't you?" He folded his arms and gave her a firm stare.

"Maybe."

"Don't insult my intelligence, you knew what he'd done and chose to take advantage of his naivety. That was a very immature thing to do, not to mention dangerous. I want you to leave me alone for five minutes while I sort out Cadmus and calm down." He turned his back on her and without further ado Aldara left the camp.

As Nicodemus busied himself getting Cadmus cleaned up, he felt his own stomach churning; he figured it was just a reaction to Cadmus being ill and was pleasantly distracted by Ximena returning with Tyrone, having successfully stocked up on food and fresh water. Gladly, she shared the water with Cadmus and helped Nicodemus put him to bed to 'sleep it off'.

"Are you alright Unc? You look nearly as rough as Cadmus."

"I'm sure I'll be alright in a minute. It's just that looking after people being sick always makes me feel ill too. If you don't mind, I need to go and speak to Opehlia and Aldara."

"Go for it. I'll sort out some supper for us."

It was Aldara whom Nicodemus found first. He really wasn't in the mood for long lectures and punishments so he just explained that she had been very silly and had put Cadmus and the mission in jeopardy. She did look genuinely sorry, so he finished by telling her she must apologise to the others and work twice as hard in future if she was going to help them get to Delos.

Now for the hard part…

"Hi Phe, I thought I'd find you here," Nicodemus said as he reached the top of the wall and found Ophelia nestled deep inside the petals of a pretty little flower.

"Don't try and sweet talk me, Nicodemus—I warned you. It's them or me!"

Nicodemus had seen her like this before and knew it was fruitless to try and get her to change her mind; only now he had to decide what to do. If he told Cadmus and Aldara to leave, it would be going against Pia's advice; but if he didn't, he would lose his best friend. Not a choice I would like to make, I can tell you. Nicodemus made his decision.

"Ophelia, you know you mean the world to me, but Pia told me I would need the man from the east to help rescue Thaddea and I can't ignore this. I implore you to stay with me. We've been through worse before. Please, if not for me, then for Thaddea."

"Nicodemus, I meant what I said. If you insist on letting Cadmus and Aldara stay, then you leave me no choice. I love you dearly but cannot sit idly by and watch you destroy your daughter's chances of survival. I must leave you now, old friend—I'm sorry it has to end this way but I think you are making a grave mistake."

Nicodemus could do nothing but watch helplessly as his friend took off into the sunset. As he climbed back down to the cave his guts wrenched with pain. He just put this down to his current situation.

"You have every right to be angry with me."

Chapter 10

Commitment to Friendship

Ximena was having trouble sleeping, desperately trying to work out how they were going to make any progress. Cadmus would undoubtedly have a thumping hangover and would be next to useless, and without Ophelia, Tyronne and Aldara would have to take it in turns carrying two people, and Nicodemus was no lightweight. Her scrambled thoughts were disturbed, by some awful moaning coming from the darkness. Cadmus sobering up, she assumed, until…

"Phe, where are you? Phe, I'm sorry, please come back."

Ximena grabbed her torch, threw on her jumper and found her way over to Nicodemus. She knelt down next to him. She knew he was having a distressing dream and didn't want to startle him, so gently put one hand on his back to comfort him. To her shock he was burning up, and his shirt was saturated with sweat. She racked her brains to think what medicines they had with them. She was just on her way back to her belongings when Nicodemus reached out to her.

"Ximena, you have to help me, I think I'm dying."

"Nicodemus, don't say such things! You'll be fine. It's probably just a reaction to everything that's happened lately. Let me get my things. I'm bound to have something that'll bring your temperature down and then you'll feel much better." As she crept past Cadmus, Ximena decided that it might be sensible to wake him; he may not be much use to her but if Nicodemus was really ill she might need him to get help.

"Ow, my head hurts!" he complained as he came round.

"We haven't got time for that! There's something seriously wrong with Nicodemus—he's burning up and says he's dying."

Cadmus, forgetting his own troubles, leapt up and went straight over.

"What's wrong Nicodemus, where does it hurt."

"It's my stomach. The pain's dreadful—I can't stand it."

"Here, take one of these, it should help." Ximena handed Nicodemus a couple of pills and the water canister.

"Thank you." Nicodemus took the pills but within a matter of minutes he was bent double in agony.

"God, what do you think's wrong with him, Cadmus?"

"I don't know."

"I thought you were clever." Ximena's concerns were making her snappy.

"I am, or at least I know a lot of useless trivia, but I'm not a doctor. I don't have all the answers, Ximena. Please don't get cross with me. I know you're worried but I'm here to help, remember?"

Before Ximena could answer, Nicodemus let out an excruciating roar and then he, too, was violently sick.

"Do you think he's been drinking too?" Cadmus asked.

"No, you idiot, he has not been drinking. Look, why don't you go and get Aldara and perhaps you could try and do something useful like finding Ophelia."

Cadmus didn't bother to answer. He just quietly gathered a few bits together and left. Clearly he was just a burden and perhaps it would be better if he and Aldara did leave.

Aldara had said she was going to sleep out of the camp that night because she had already caused enough trouble. Cadmus spotted her exquisite colours glistening in the moonlight, while she slept peacefully, curled up in some dried up leaves, near the entrance of the cave.

"Time to wake up, beautiful," he whispered softly.

"Hey you, what's happening? It's still dark."

"It's Nicodemus. He's sick and we need to go and find Ophelia." Cadmus was very solemn and could hardly bring himself to look at Aldara.

"There's more to it than that, Cadmus. I know you too well. Come on, out with it."

"I think we're causing too many problems for Nicodemus. He has enough on his plate trying to get to Delos without us messing everything up. Once we've found Ophelia we ought to leave."

"I'm sorry, this is all my fault. I should never have let you drink that Ouzo and I certainly shouldn't have brought you back to the camp when you were drunk. I'll make it up to you, I promise; you go back and help Ximena—I'll find Ophelia and smooth things out."

"Are you sure that's a good idea? She's quite a force to be reckoned with."

"It's time I grew up, Cadmus, and there is no time like the present. Now go before I change my mind."

Reluctantly Cadmus left Aldara and went back to the cave. Once inside he could see things had not improved. "Aldara has gone to find Ophelia and when she returns we'll leave you in peace. Is there anything you want me to do in the meantime?" Cadmus didn't imagine for one minute that Ximena would want him around but thought it only common courtesy to offer.

"Oh Cadmus, there's no need to leave. I'm so sorry; I shouldn't have treated you like that. If Larissa was here she'd have given me a serious talking to. She's forever telling me I'm too rude to people. I wish she was here now; apart from the fact I miss her terribly, she's really good when people are ill—not like me: I just get grumpy."

"Do you have any idea what's wrong yet? Nicodemus still looks dreadful."

"In between bouts of sickness he did manage to tell me that earlier on he'd pigged out on a burger he'd found down a drain. I suppose that could be causing it."

"Sounds like food poisoning to me. We'll just have to sit it out, but it will leave him very weak. Have you been able to get his temperature down yet?"

"No, he's thrown up everything he's taken; he can't even hold down water at the moment."

"Okay, we'll just have to look after him the best we can. Oh, and thanks."

"For what?" Ximena was still a bit preoccupied with Nicodemus to have full attention on their conversation.

"For your apology—I'm sorry too. Do you think we can all start afresh?"

"That's fine with me, but I think a lot will depend on Ophelia." Ximena gave Cadmus an uncertain smile.

"Let's hope Aldara can work her magic then."

"Let's just worry about looking after Nicodemus, shall we?"

"Yes boss!" Cadmus had managed to relax a bit and was very relieved to have Ximena's forgiveness. Together they set about making Nicodemus as comfortable as possible.

Meanwhile Aldara had been flying all over the place in search of Ophelia, screaming her name at the top of her voice and that was pretty loud, believe me. Yet still she had not found her. She stopped to catch her breath and slumped down on a rock. Her wings drooped down by her sides and her head hung heavily, portraying her feelings of despair. How was she going to find her? She could be anywhere by now. It was moments like this that she envied people's ability to cry; she had no way of relieving her angst, so instead she gave one final hellish yell.

"Ophelia, where are you?"

"Right behind you—there's no need to shout."

Aldara nearly fell off the rock. "Oh thank God—I thought I was never going to find you! You must come back. Nicodemus is very sick and we don't know what to do."

"Why am I not surprised?" Ophelia said sarcastically.

"You have every right to be angry with me, Ophelia, but can we please just put our differences aside? Nicodemus really needs you with him now. Besides, Cadmus and I have agreed to leave if you come back."

Unexpectedly, Ophelia was not happy to hear this news but was instead awash with guilt. Although Cadmus and Aldara had behaved badly, they were still young, so what was her excuse? Really, she should have been leading by example and not running away at the first hurdle. Although not quite ready to divulge this revelation, she answered, "I don't think any of us should be making any rash decisions right now, so I suggest we just hurry up and get back to the others. We can sort everything else out later."

Not wishing to tempt fate, Aldara kept quiet and followed Ophelia. Together, guided by the light of the moon, they flew back to the cave.

By the time they arrived Nicodemus was beginning to feel a little bit better; he hadn't been sick for a while and had taken some tablets that were steadily bringing his temperature down.

"Phe, I'm so glad to see you! I missed you, old friend." Nicodemus tried to sit up to greet her.

"Time for you to rest, old man, I'm here now and not going anywhere. We'll talk in the morning."

Nicodemus did not have the energy to argue and was just grateful that the sickness had eased and his fever was going. He lay back down and closed his eyes. His thoughts were filled with joy that Ophelia had returned. This was a good omen—everything would be fine now, wouldn't it?

“I can’t do this anymore.”

Chapter 11

Diomede's Defiance

As daylight broke the sun shone through the leaves of the tree they had taken refuge in, casting a stream of light across Diomede and Ulysses as they slept recovering from yet another flight across from Delos. Diomede was exhausted, not only from the three consecutive trips he had endured but also from the constant barrage of abuse he received from his mother. He had been quite enjoying the warmth of the rays until he remembered what it was he was doing there. This instantly put him in a bad mood.

"I can't do this anymore, Ulysses—I've had enough. My mother is a cruel woman and although it pains me to say so, I no longer wish to have anything to do with her."

"I understand your pain, Diomede. I've watched you suffer under the vicious tongue of your mother for too long now. Together we can make a stand, you know. I too have had enough. I'm not designed to attack all the time. I'm only meant to defend my home, not like those dreadful hornets—they take delight in harming others. I simply can't stand them. I don't want to harm that sweet butterfly! She's done us no wrong and is already badly hurt. I would rather go back and fight Perseus than carry out this assassination."

"I couldn't have said it better myself, Ulysses, but taking on my mother is easier said than done. And that's not all." Diomede went quiet.

"Yes, and…"

"It's Cleopatra. I think I'm falling in love with her and my mother would never allow it."

"Not one for doing things by halves, are you, mate!"

"Yeah, great, isn't it?"

"So what's so special about Cleopatra?"

"Well, you've seen her, haven't you?"

"Yes, and I'm a Tropical Wasp, so what's your point?"

"Oh, I see what you mean. Well, to me she's totally gorgeous! Her immaculate pale skin against the warm chestnut glow of her hair is enough to melt me, and as for those steely grey eyes—well, they just leave me speechless." Diomede's eyes glazed over with a dreamy expression.

Ulysses chuckled. "Oh dear, you have got it bad, haven't you? So what exactly to you propose to do about it?"

"Well, there's my dilemma; firstly, I have to tell my mother I have no intention of living with her anymore, and then I have to convince Cleopatra that despite having done many bad things, I've changed and want to help her and her father."

"Piece of cake."

"Yes, thanks for your support, pal! But seriously, how am I going to handle this?"

"I have an idea."

"No more jokes, Ulysses. This is for real, you know."

"Trust me, you're going to like this. Now listen carefully…"

Diomede and Ulysses spent some considerable length of time discussing their plan of action and when they were finally satisfied they decided there was no time like the present. As he boarded his greatest friend, Diomede said, "If we don't make it through this I just want to thank you for helping me do the right thing. I've spent my life in my mother's shadow and it's time I stood up for myself. So as the three musketeers would say, "One for all and all for one!" And so they set off.

“Don’t worry, I’ve eaten.”

Chapter 12

Golden Burial

It was a good 24 hours before Nicodemus was ready to continue his quest and, despite still being weak and having not managed to eat anything other than dry bread, he was not prepared to wait any longer.

"We need to get a few things sorted before we go any further," he declared to the others. "If we stand any hope of rescuing Thaddea and Larissa, we need to stop fighting amongst ourselves and concentrate our efforts on how we are going to conquer Acantha and her army." Everyone began to look about shiftily. "Ophelia, you need to agree to do your best to get along with Cadmus and Aldara. I know they're young and prone to get into trouble, but they have good hearts and are here to help."

Ophelia ruffled her fur, took a deep breath ready to protest, opened her mouth to speak but, instead, thought better of it and just nodded her head in acceptance.

"And you two," Nicodemus cast his gaze across to Cadmus and Aldara, "you must promise to be on your best behaviour from now on. Without Ophelia we won't succeed, and apart from that she is my best friend in the world and I've lost enough already without losing her. I'm not going to say anymore, other than I expect what I have said to be taken on board and adhered to. So with the lecture over and done with, let's go and rescue my daughter."

Relieved to be staying, Cadmus and Aldara were the first in the air, followed shortly by Ximena on Tyrone and, bringing up the rear, Nicodemus and Ophelia. They still had quite a way to go before reaching the town of Chora and agreed that due to Nicodemus' fragile state, they would stop regularly to rest and rejuvenate.

After a few hours and a couple of non-eventful stops they had made good headway. They decided to take a final stop before reaching Chora and head towards some trees that were growing on the edge of a secluded part of the beach. After everyone had dismounted, Ophelia, Tyrone and Aldara flew off in search of some suitable refreshments, leaving the others to settle down for a bite to eat and a rest in the coolness of the tree.

They were merrily chatting and eating, when Ximena got a prickly sensation that they were being watched. She excused herself to have a look around but couldn't see anything. She was just making her way back to her seat when she spotted something on one of the branches. As she crept forward to take a closer look she shuddered at what she saw.

Slumped lifelessly across one of the leaves was Vanessa, Larissa's butterfly. Her abdomen had swollen to unrecognisable proportions and her once vibrant and powerful wings had been reduced to tattered and torn remnants; their colour drained and weak, showing no signs of their original beauty.

Ximena's heart froze, as did she, temporarily. Then taking a deep breath and preparing herself for the worst, she gingerly approached. Carefully she crouched down to see if Vanessa was still breathing. Thankfully, she was. She whispered softly, "Vanessa, it's me, Ximena—can you hear me?" She felt her throat constricting and her eyes filling with tears. She strained to hear the faint reply.

"Thank God you're here. Is Nicodemus with you?" Vanessa was very short of breath and wheezing terribly.

"Yes, he is. Shall I get him for you?"

"I don't want you to leave me now, I'm scared I think I'm dying."

Ximena was having great difficulty holding herself together. This was the second time in as many days that one of her friends had told her they were dying—only this time she believed it to be true. She reached out her hand to touch Vanessa; the swelling had spread to her face and all her pretty delicate features had been obscured. She felt her fingers singe as the heat from Vanessa's skin came into contact with them. "What happened to you?" she asked tentatively.

"One of Acantha's hornets stung me and the poison has spread through my body. I don't know how long I've got, but I must speak with Nicodemus. If you call out to him do you think he will hear?" It hurt Vanessa to talk; everywhere felt tender and sore, her vision was becoming distorted, filled with tiny dots of light. Perhaps they were stars from heaven that she could see.

Ximena cupped her hands around her mouth and shouted, "Nicodemus, come quickly! I've found Vanessa!" Taking a huge gasp for more air, she added, "We're over to your left, amongst the leaves." She looked down at her friend whose breathing was very shallow and intermittent. It seemed ages before the response came.

"Hang on, we're on our way." The familiar sound of Nicodemus was reassuring and Ximena was grateful that she hadn't had to leave Vanessa.

Nicodemus and Cadmus appeared in no time at all and the look on Ximena's face explained everything. There was no need for words. Nicodemus swapped places with Ximena and sat beside Vanessa who stirred slightly and then asked, "Nicodemus, is that you?"

"Yes little one, it's me. I'm so sorry you've been hurt. Is there anything we can do to make you more comfortable?"

"No, thank you; most of my body has become numb now, so please don't worry about me. I have good news for you, though." Vanessa's eyes glazed over and she was drifting away.

"Vanessa, stay with me! What's your news?"

"Sorry, it's Thaddea—she's alive and with Larissa. They're being held…" Her voice was so quiet now Nicodemus didn't hear the last bit.

"Vanessa my love, I'm sorry to have to ask you to speak. I know it's hard but where did you say they were being held?"

"In a... In a dungeon inside a large... a large well."

"You've done so well, little one, you rest now." Nicodemus didn't know what to do and then Vanessa said,

"Nicodemus... please sing to me and please... tell Larissa I love her."

Nicodemus knew what he should do now and suggested to Cadmus and Ximena that they leave him and Vanessa alone. Mournfully they left. Cadmus gently put his arm around Ximena as the tears finally broke down the barriers and flowed down her cheeks.

Nicodemus subtly cleared his throat that had become quite lumpy from emotion and with Vanessa's head nestling on his lap he looked down on her. Her eyes were motionless but he could still see warmth and love in them. Lovingly he started to sing to her. He chose a beautiful lullaby that he had sung many times to Thaddea to help her sleep. Nicodemus had become lost in his own world of singing and thoughts of Thaddea, so it was some time before he realised that the warmth coming from Vanessa's body was waning and, as he looked down on her once more, he saw that she had slipped away peacefully and was no longer suffering.

Nicodemus was struck with grief once more. How right Pia had been when she said the journey was going to be fraught with danger and that he would want to go back to the safety and comfort of his own home. How he longed to see her beautiful face and feel her body entwined with his. As the reality that this could never happen filled his thoughts he let out a sad sigh and breathed, "I miss you, my love." Nicodemus was not going to be able to dwell in his own sadness for long, for soon Cadmus and Ximena returned and with them, Ophelia, Aldara and Tyrone.

"I'm sorry about Vanessa," Nicodemus said to Ximena.

"Me too—poor Larissa, she'll be heartbroken. I hope she's okay. She's not exactly cut out for this sort of thing." She was about to go on to say not that anyone could really be, when she got that prickly sensation again; hesitantly, she turned around, instantly wishing she hadn't. Speechless, she tapped Cadmus on the shoulder and pointed in the direction of the larger-than-life reason for the prickly sensation that had overwhelmed her. His jaw dropped and the colour drained from his cheeks. He gulped and was just going to yell 'RUN!' when the new arrival said:

"Don't worry, I've eaten, I just wanted to know if I could offer my help, I couldn't help hearing your sad news."

These kind words were a huge relief to everyone because, standing in front of them, was a giant Golden Silk Spider. (Giant to them, of course; you have to remember they are no bigger than your thumb!) Admittedly, she was stunning! Her body was a rich tan colour sprayed with yellow dots. Her long legs, all eight of them, were black and tan with wonderful feathery tufts on her knees, or at least her equivalent to our knees.

"That's very kind of you," Nicodemus managed. "May I ask how would you be able to help us?"

"If it's okay with you, I'd like to spin a coffin for your friend; then you can give her a proper burial."

"That's a lovely idea," Ximena smiled. "I know Larissa would want her to have the best possible burial. Thank you so much."

Together they all watched while the spider worked her magic. Her legs moved with speed and elegance, spinning and weaving incredible yellow silk threads around Vanessa's body. When she was finished she stepped backwards to allow the sun to shine down on her finery. There, before them, lay a beautiful golden cocoon, a coffin fit for royalty. Carefully, they picked it up and slowly walked towards a small hole in the bark of the tree. Gently they placed Vanessa, in her golden shroud, inside the hole. They gathered some leaves and covered the hole. Nicodemus said a few words and they all bowed their heads in prayer.

Happy that Vanessa had now received a worthy burial, Ximena turned to the spider. "You've been very generous. Is there anything we can do for you?"

"I think there might be, but firstly I must explain a few things to you." The spider relaxed into a comfortable position, much like a grown up getting ready to read a story to a nursery class. "My name is Metis and I live in Florida…"

"Wow, how did you get here?" Cadmus interrupted.

"I expect Metis will tell us, if you can manage to keep quiet," Ophelia pointed out in the nicest tone possible, so Nicodemus didn't think she was causing problems.

"Oh yes, sorry, please go on," said Cadmus.

"Well, you see, the thing is, I've always wanted to know why my mum gave me a Greek name; but unfortunately she died before I ever got the chance to ask."

Cadmus was just going to ask what happened to her when Aldara gave him a quick jab in the ribs and he thought perhaps he'd wait until Metis had finished.

"So I decided to come to Greece and do some investigating for myself. Your Islands are very popular with the Americans—they love to learn about your history. Their country is so new in comparison to yours. For instance, the oldest house in Florida is in a place called St Augustine. It was built in 1723, making it only a few hundred years old. " (I know this is true because I've been there!) "Unlike the ruins found here, which I understand are thousands of years old."

"That's right," Cadmus interjected. "The Terrace of Lions on Delos was built 600BC" (been there too!), "and did you know that they were dedicated to Apollo, who was born there, by the people of Naxos?"

Metis took a minute to adjust her position. I think she was enjoying all the attention! She continued, "No, I didn't, so thank you—and now back to how I got here; I overheard the humans who live in my house—well, actually it's their house but I live there too, anyway—they were saying that they were coming to Greece for their holiday, so I waited for the opportune moment and when the suitcase was open and no one was around I sneakily crawled inside and waited for the lid to close. When the case was opened again I found myself here."

Cadmus glanced at Ophelia and with a nod of approval, he proceeded with the words, "If I may be so bold," and he stepped a little closer to the rather intimidating creature. "I think your story is a great one and what an adventure you must have had to come all this way. There are actually many reasons why your mother gave you a Greek name, so in no particular order I shall begin." It was now Cadmus' chance to be centre stage, "Firstly, the scientific name for a Spider is *Arachnid* and it comes from the Greek story about a girl named Arachne who loved to weave. Her weaving was so beautiful and perfect that the goddess Athena got jealous and, to punish her, she turned her into a spider. However, this did not deter Arachne and she continued to weave for the rest of her life."

"Gosh, I never knew that!" Ophelia said.

"Now who's interrupting?" Cadmus said with a cheeky smile.

"Do excuse me, young man, please continue," she replied with a giggle.

"Thank you, I will. In addition to this you may wish to know that your Greek name is Nephila Clavipes and the word Nephila means 'fond of spinning'; and finally, yes, there's more"—he was definitely enjoying this and for the first time Ophelia softened and realised there was more to him than met the eye, or in her case, five eyes. "I believe you have given great honour to the name 'Metis' because it means wisdom and skill, both of which you have in abundance." And with that he took a small bow and went back to his seat. Those in the audience who were able to clap did and the others let out small cheers.

"That's fascinating, thank you. I've always liked my name but it feels particularly special now I know more about it. I think it's time for me to do some more exploring. It was lovely to meet you all and I wish you the best of luck in your travels." After everyone said their goodbyes Metis crawled off as quietly as when she had arrived, leaving the six friends to gather their things and take flight once more.

Her wings were entangled in her uncontrollable
flaming red hair.

Chapter 13

Friend or Foe?

Feeling drained and exhausted from the day's events they eventually reached Chora town.

"Time to restock our supplies, everyone," Nicodemus said as they all landed on a rooftop. "And do we think we could be a bit more careful this time?" he added. (In my opinion, he should have known better than to say things like that!)

They arranged to go off in their pairs and meet up later to find somewhere to settle for the night. Ophelia dropped Nicodemus off near some bins at the back of a restaurant and told him to choose wisely this time. Then she went off in search of some sweet nectar for her tea.

Nicodemus was carefully picking through some leftover bread when out of nowhere came the most beautiful fairy he had ever seen. Her wings were entangled in her uncontrollable flaming red hair that flew about like Medusa's snakes. (Come to think of it, Athena punished Medusa as well as Arachne.) Her intense green eyes shone with the radiance of emeralds and her pearl white skin was sprinkled with freckles. He felt as if he had been turned to stone like one of Medusa's victims and that his feet had been welded to the ground beneath them.

"Good evening, Nicodemus, how are you feeling today?" Her voice was enchanting and Nicodemus was reminded of the first time Pia had spoken to him, which prompted him to ask; "How did you know my name?"

"Not even hello? I'm disappointed, Nicodemus—I'd heard such great things about you!"

"You're right, that was rude! Good evening to you too, and I'm feeling quite well today, thank you. As you know my name, may I ask yours?"

"That's better, and certainly you may ask. My name is Celosia, and your darling wife has sent me to watch over you. She had heard of your illness and was concerned for your well being." (As she spoke Celosia craftily crossed her fingers behind her back.)

"Pia? Have you spoken to her?"

"Not in person, but I was sent a message from our highest order, so I knew you must be important." She flashed a twinkling smile.

"Goodness, I am honoured."

"It is I that am honoured, and I beseech you to fly with me and grace the other fairies with your presence."

"That would be lovely, but I must just tell Ophelia where I'm going."

"That's all taken care of. I've already spoken to her and she said to have fun and she would see you later.

"Right." Nicodemus suddenly had a thought. "How will I get there without Ophelia?"

"Honestly, Nicodemus, do you know nothing about fairies? We are gifted with tremendous strength and it would be my pleasure to escort you." Celosia spread out her long elegant arms but Nicodemus was still welded to his ledge. "It's quite safe, you know, and you might even like it. Just relax and I'll take care of everything."

Prudently, Nicodemus edged his way into her arms. She had the fragrance of a fresh spring meadow and the touch of a newborn baby as it takes hold of your finger for the first time. Nicodemus thought perhaps he'd died and gone to heaven—until he looked down and saw the ground moving beneath his feet. He flinched nervously but Celosia's arms closed in tightly around him. It was nice to feel the arms of a woman round him again; he was just sorry they were not Pia's. Before he had too much time to feel melancholy his thoughts were interrupted.

"Here we are, safe and sound," Celosia said as she landed gracefully in the most fascinating tree Nicodemus had ever seen. The trunk looked like hundreds of faces had been carved out of the knotted bark and it oozed authority and wisdom. He wondered if perhaps inside all its haunting twists and turns this tree held all the answers; he yearned to reach into the hollows and put it to the test. Celosia had left him to find the other fairies and during that brief time he wished Cadmus was there to tell him all about fairies and what the name Celosia meant, although he felt sure it would mean something along the lines of 'The most beautiful and enchanting Goddess'. It was unfortunate for Nicodemus that Cadmus wasn't there because if he had been he would have told him that Celosia means 'Burning Flame' and then would have suggested that they flee before things got too hot to handle.

Therefore, completely ignorant of his fate and still under the blissful illusion that they were there to watch over him, he was ecstatic to see an influx of fairies, all as endearing as Celosia. Nicodemus was in his element chatting and laughing, totally unaware that their existence was intoxicating him, until he suddenly felt overcome with tiredness and his body was becoming numb. He tried to move his legs but he couldn't. He started to panic when he came to the frightening conclusion that these fairies were not there to help him but were in fact 'Sylvans'—the evil tree fairies that Pia had warned him about when she had appeared in the fireplace. What was it she had told him to do? He racked his brains and then he remembered… That's it! The iron bracelet, which he had brought for protection. Fat lot of good that was going to do him now, for it was in Ophelia's saddlebag. He was rapidly losing consciousness and could not move his body at all. Finally he succumbed and closed his eyes. Instead of the sound of silence that he had expected, he was aware of a lot of noise and confusion and then of a sudden weightlessness; perhaps this was what rising up to heaven felt like, he pondered.

Abruptly, he felt a tremendous slap across his face. "Nicodemus, wake up!" Ximena screamed at him. "Is this your idea of being careful? What were you thinking! Don't you ever go off with anyone without telling one of us first."

"Good to see you too, sweetheart." Nicodemus was barely compos mentis but was still able to wind his niece up with some sarcasm.

"It's not funny, you know, I was worried sick."

No longer under the wicked spell, Nicodemus was coming round quite quickly. "How did you get me away from them?"

"When we realised you'd gone we figured the Sylvans had taken you. They usually lure people into the forest but fortunately for us there aren't many trees in Chora, so we didn't have too much trouble finding you. Then it was simply a case of thrusting the iron bracelet at them and they all vanished. We grabbed you and brought you here. And Uncle, if you don't mind me saying so, you could do with losing a few pounds—you weigh a tonne."

"Sorry love, not just for being too heavy but for putting your life at risk as well as mine. I shall practise what I preach in future." Nicodemus had managed to get all the feeling back in his body now and although feeling a bit sleepy had made a full recovery.

"I don't wish to put a downer on this happy reunion," Ophelia put in, "but I don't know how long the fairies will stay away, so I suggest we make haste. Are you fit enough to fly, old friend?" Ophelia had been very quiet up until then. I think it had come as quite a shock to her that Nicodemus had been in such danger.

"Yes, I think so. I could probably do with a leg up, though, if that's alright." He breathed in to try and look thinner. Ximena gave a quick snigger and then helped her uncle up onto Ophelia's back.

"Where are the others?" Nicodemus asked as they took off.

"I suggested to Cadmus that he and Aldara do circuits around the area to keep watch until we got you to safety."

"I'm glad things are all sorted out between you. I think we have a good team now and Acantha had better be on her guard." No sooner had he said this, when he had an unexpected relapse and was no longer able to keep himself upright. He lost his balance and before Ophelia knew what was happening he had fallen from the saddle.

Plummeting through the air, Nicodemus could see the ground coming ever closer. In those split seconds his life flashed before him. The experiences of the last few days had taught him more about friendship than he had ever thought possible. The question, now, was whether or not he would live long enough to enjoy it.

Out of nowhere, pelting through the air like a bullet, came Aldara, known for being one of the fastest flying insects in the world. If anyone could save Nicodemus, she could.

"Gotcha!" she said with a groan, as Nicodemus landed with a wallop on her back. His weight caused her to drop dramatically and they were hardly more than a foot off the ground by the time she was level again.

"Thanks Aldara, I owe you one."

"All in a day's work, big guy. Now shall we go and find the others?"

"Please." Nicodemus didn't have the energy for anything else and was really very keen to put his feet down on something that wasn't moving.

“Catch this!” came a life-saving voice from above..

Chapter 14

Night of Terror

Reunited once more and having had a short rest and a refuel, the weary travellers decided to turn in for the night. There were no more boats making the crossing to Delos that day and it looked as though a storm was blowing in. The sky had been hijacked by menacing black clouds and the friends were being brutally blown about by the wind.

While they were flying towards the port, to find refuge in one of the church roofs, the heavens opened and they were caught in a torrential downpour. The raindrops were enormous and bitterly cold. Terrifyingly, the sky exploded with bolts of lightning, fighting their way to the ground, followed by deafening claps of thunder. The ground appeared to shake with the noise and it was soon agreed by all that they must quickly find shelter before something else awful happened.

It was Tyrone who spotted the tiny footbridge (tiny for us, that is) beneath them and, although not ideal, it was not a bad option considering that little else was available to them and time was not on their side. They flew down and were soon enjoying the protection of the bridge, although the wind was still blowing under it; their size meant they could crawl up in between the bricks where some of the mortar had worn away. It was actually quite snug; they all managed to find good places to get comfy and, remarkably, drifted off in no time at all. Personally, if I'd had a day like theirs I would have done so as well.

Ximena was having another restless night. She longed for her home comforts; warm bed, cuddly duvet and puffed pillows, not to mention her floral pyjamas. Most of all, she wanted her bathroom. As much as she fancied herself as an outdoor kind of girl, prepared to do almost anything, there comes a point when you get a bit tired of finding the girls' bathroom behind a hedge—if you know what I mean! Blearily, she opened one eye, the other one still stuck together with sleep. The lightning was still flashing violently, illuminating the night sky and their temporary campsite. As she glanced round checking everyone was okay, she realised there weren't enough bodies bundled in the crevices. Impatiently she rubbed the sleep from her closed eye to be sure her vision had not been obscured, but sure enough, someone was missing. 'Why did everything keep going wrong?' she thought. Was this punishment for her being rude in the past? If it were, she vowed never to be rude again in the vain hope that they might get through the rest of the journey without any more disasters. (She might as well have bought a lottery ticket. I think the odds of winning would have been higher than the chances of them having no more disasters!)

"Everyone wake up, someone's missing!"

There were grumbles and groans from all directions as everyone began to surface.

"Uh, what's all the fuss?" Cadmus murmured sleepily.

"Who is it? Who's gone?" was Nicodemus' response.

"It's Tyrone," Ophelia said. "I can't see him anywhere."

"I'll go look," Aldara said, springing into action.

"Now just hang on a minute, no one is going zooming off out into that weather," Nicodemus ordered. "When was the last time anyone saw …" But before he could finish they were interrupted by shouts of,

"Help, help me! I'm down here." Tyrone was being swept along the gully below, in a furious surge of water.

"We'll go," Cadmus said bravely and he launched himself onto Aldara and they disappeared before the others had even had a chance to wish them good luck, or try and stop them.

"I can't stand this!" Ximena ranted. "He's my friend—I should be going after him."

"Come on, I'll take you," Ophelia offered, "and you'll have to come too," she added to Nicodemus, "I can't seem to leave you for five minutes without you getting into some kind of mischief."

"As long as you are happy you can carry us both," he said in reply.

"You let me worry about that. Now come on, we're wasting valuable time."

The three of them ventured into the storm. The visibility was terrible and Ophelia was finding it nearly impossible to support the weight of two people and fight the relentless wind. At an appropriate moment the sky shone like a torch, as yet more lightning struck and a short way in front of them they saw Tyrone thrashing about despairingly. Thankfully, just above him were Aldara and Cadmus. In spite of everything Nicodemus couldn't help but admire Aldara's splendour. She really was an aerodynamic masterpiece, as Cadmus had said. Her agility in the air was phenomenal; she demonstrated such strength and precision, which she had already used to save him and now, he hoped, would be able to use it to save Tyrone too. Not only that, she was lit up like an angel with a glistening aura surrounding her and Cadmus. He snapped out of his admiration by Ximena yelling at the top of her voice:

"Cadmus, look over there!"

"What? I can't hear you," was the maddening response.

Ximena persisted, "Over *there*, the rubbish floating downstream."

"Yes, I see it."

"Tell Tyrone to swim to it."

"Okay," Cadmus answered, gave Tyrone the message and then he and Aldara flew on further to see how far they had to go before the water subsided.

Fortunately the flow of the water was slowing slightly as it collected leaves and other debris in its path and Ophelia was finally getting closer.

“I tell you what, Nicodemus,” she panted, “if we get through this ordeal alive we’re both going on a diet, do you hear me!”

Before he could answer Ximena propelled herself off the saddle. As she plunged into the water below and spun sharply like a corkscrew, Nicodemus held his breath as she nearly got sucked into a swirling black hole. Fortunately she just missed it and powered her way through the water and reached a broken polystyrene cup that was bobbing about awkwardly. I think it must have been pure determination, but somehow she pulled herself up onto it. Still inside it was the plastic stirrer, which she used to paddle her way over to Tyrone who was weakening rapidly, the weight of his shell pulling him under.

“Hang on, I’m coming.” But as she got to him she realised there was no way she would be able to drag him from the water. She was nearly in tears—how could she be this close and fail? She felt useless and each time Tyrone went under the water he took longer to resurface.

“Catch this!” came a life-saving voice from above.

As Ximena looked up, she caught sight of Nicodemus’ rope swinging in the air. She reached up and grabbed hold of it, being careful not to tip herself back into the water. She tugged it so he knew she had a good grip. With Ophelia doing her best to hover, Nicodemus slowly offered up some slack so Ximena could tie the rope around Tyrone. The only trouble was, Tyrone wasn’t strong enough to support his own weight for long periods of time, so once again Ximena threw herself into the water. She swam right underneath Tyrone, dragging the rope behind her and at the same time wrapping it around his middle. Once she'd finished and clambered back into her makeshift raft her hopes were dashed for a second time. When she tried throwing the rope back up to Nicodemus, the wind blew it out of the way so he couldn't catch it. It was an agonising experience for all of them; Ophelia's fur was completely waterlogged, adding dreadfully to the already exhausting weight, and Nicodemus was beginning to suffer terribly from the severe beating he was sustaining from the wind. Just when they feared they would lose another dear friend, Aldara returned; she was flying upside down with Cadmus hanging gallantly from his saddle with his arms dangling and hands outstretched.

"Pass me the rope," he instructed.

All Ximena's anxieties vanished. She was really impressed by Cadmus—he wasn't just as academic after all. She held out the rope and he snatched it as they sped past; then, in one nifty manoeuvre, Aldara did a 360 turn, ground to a halt and then backed up to join Ophelia.

"Thank God you're here," Nicodemus said. "Can you pull him out by yourself or do you need a hand?"

"No, I can manage—get yourselves to safety," Aldara replied.

Nicodemus was in no hurry to argue with that and headed off to some safer terrain, while Cadmus wrapped the rope round him, fastened himself to Aldara, and then gave the command.

"Heave!"

Initially nothing happened and Aldara wondered if sending Nicodemus away had been a good idea, but after a few unwavering efforts Tyrone's body was on the move, Ximena, in the water for the third time now, was not feeling cold any longer. The adrenaline had kicked in and she had a sudden rush of energy, just enough to help guide Tyrone to the edge of the gully and out of the water. She collapsed into a heap next to him, half laughing, half crying. He hadn't spoken to her yet, but then he was a beetle of very few words (well, I don't know that for sure; it may have just been that Ximena chatted so much he couldn't get a word in edgeways); but she knew he was okay because he had given her that look of thanks that conveyed more than a thousand words without saying a single one.

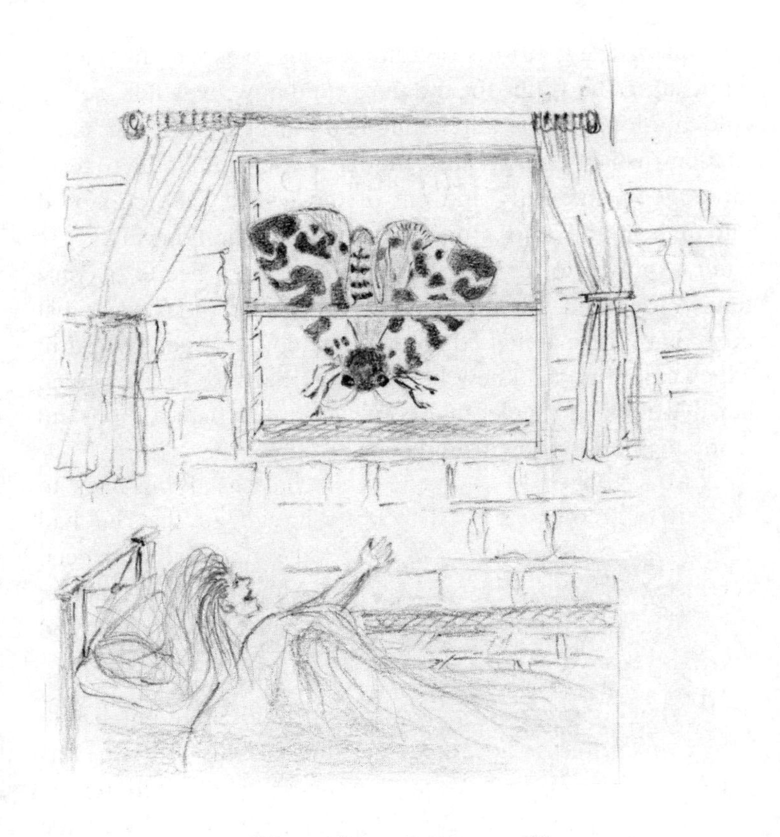

“How did you escape?”

Chapter 15

The Traitor Returns

Unbeknownst to Diomede while he was flying back to Delos, empowered with the knowledge that he had chosen not to harm Vanessa, she had sadly died and been ceremoniously buried by her friends. Although, I do believe, even if he had been aware of it, he would not have altered his plans.

Having vowed, no matter how difficult it might be, to betray his mother, for the first time in his life he was experiencing true feelings of happiness. He would rescue everyone, save the day and get the girl. (I think he'd watched too many movies, but you never know!) You certainly couldn't knock him for his passion and he was going to need every ounce of it to get through the rest of the day, let alone anything else.

As soon as he arrived, he went straight to the North Tower to find Cleopatra.

"Cleopatra, it's me, Diomede." He tapped on her door and waited patiently.

"Go away! If you've come to gloat, I'm not interested." She had spent the night shut in her room weeping, while her beautiful Tiger moth Lysandra hung pitifully from that evil torture trap. Even though she had felt sorry for Diomede when his mother had been so cruel, that didn't mean she would forgive him for going to kill Vanessa.

"Please let me in, I need to speak to you." He was whispering now, just in case his mother had those awful hornet spies listening in.

"I said go away!"

Diomede slunk down onto the floor, leant his back up against the thick wooden door and plonked his head in his hands. Then he sat bolt upright and swung round. He pushed his face up close to the keyhole and said, "Cleopatra, I know you have no reason to listen to me and I'm sure if I were you I would be behaving the same way, but you must believe me when I say I did *not* kill Vanessa. Yes, I flew to Mykonos, but when I got there I didn't look for her—I couldn't do it. I don't want to be the bad guy anymore; it just doesn't feel right. Please let me in. I promise I will help you to free your father and Lysandra." Looking at him, you would definitely think he was a bit too hunky to be begging like this—but love does funny things to a person, you can take my word for it!

Finally there was a definitive click of the key and the handle turned, and a single ray of light sprung through the crack in the doorway.

"You'd better be telling the truth or I swear to God I will kill you myself." Cleopatra backed away after opening the door.

"I mean it, I've never been more serious in my life." Diomede came right up close to Cleopatra and took her hands in his. "I realise now that Larissa was right, a life without love is not worth living and I had been without love for so long that I had forgotten what it felt like—that is, until I met you." He felt his cheeks glowing but was determined to keep going; so he released her hands, moved away slightly and continued. "Meeting you was like being woken from a coma, a painful and lonely coma, and all I think about is you and how I want to be with you. I know my mother will never forgive me and I don't care anymore, this is my life and she has been ruling it for too long. She can order Zeno around from now on, he's welcome to her." He knelt down next to Cleopatra, who had sat back down in her mother's armchair. Nervously, he looked into her eyes and took her hands once more.

"Do you really mean this, Diomede?" she asked, still not convinced. "How do I know this isn't another of your mother's evil scams?"

"Quickly, you must come with me. Ulysses has gone to tell Zeno it is our turn to watch over Lysandra; once he has gone we can set her free."

"I'm giving you one chance." Together they left the North Tower.

When they got to the courtyard it appeared that Diomede had been telling the truth. Ulysses was there alone just as he had said he would be. However, as soon as they got close to Lysandra, Acantha, sat smugly in her thorny chariot, was pulled from the shadows by Danae and Perseus.

"Did you succeed?" she hissed at Diomede.

Now was his moment—he would tell her once and for all. He stepped towards her but buckled and instead of his resolve to stand up to her, said meekly, "Of course, mother, would you expect anything less from your dutiful son?" He felt such a fake; all that nonsense he had blurted out to Ulysses and Cleopatra about standing up to her, but really, he was just a gutless wonder that didn't deserve anyone's love, let alone someone as loving and trusting as Cleopatra.

"Good, now what are you doing here and why is she with you?"

Diomede couldn't bear to look at Cleopatra, he felt so ashamed. "I brought her here to tell her that Vanessa was dead and if she continued to disobey you the same would happen to her precious Tiger Moth." When he finished he just looked down at his feet and kicked the dust.

"Oh, perhaps there's hope for you yet," she said, slightly surprised, then told Danae it was time to leave.

"Do you trust your son?" Danae asked when they had gone round the corner.

"I know he's stupid but I trust him implicitly, why?"

"I'm not sure, I just thought he was acting a bit oddly."

"You worry too much. He loves his mother and wouldn't do anything to hurt me."

"Nonetheless, I think you should be careful."

"Well, I'm not really interested in what you think, am I? So just get on with pulling my chariot and leave the thinking to me." The rest of their journey was spent in silence.

Back in her room, slumped face down on her bed, Cleopatra was in floods of tears. 'I might have known, serves me right for tricking Danae and Perseus,' she thought to herself. That didn't make her feel any better though, and all those things Diomede had said to her—he had seemed so sincere. Was she really such a bad judge of character, or was it that everything that had happened had left her vulnerable and impressionable? She didn't know anything any more apart from how sad she was and how much she wished she could see her father. She heard a gentle tapping noise. "Go away, I hate you!" she cried into her pillow. The tapping continued. She leapt off the bed and was about to hurl her pillow at the door when she saw Lysandra at her bedroom window. Quickly, she flung it open to let her in.

"How did you escape?" she asked ecstatically.

"It was Diomede. He told me to tell you that everything he said to you was true and he was sorry for being such a coward."

"Oh dear, poor man. Come, we must find him and he can take me to father." Cleopatra gathered together a few things, climbed aboard Lysandra and they flew out of the window, leaving it slightly open, just in case they needed to get back in later. (The way things had been going, I would say that was a very good idea, wouldn't you?)

“I’m Pedros Junior—nice to meet you.”

Chapter 16

Nicodemus meets Pedros

Having managed to get back to the footbridge and their belongings, Nicodemus and the others had done their best to get back to sleep so they might regain some energy ready for the trip across to Delos in the morning. Nicodemus was the first to wake, hoping the weather had calmed down enough so that the tourist boats would be running. His ears only brought him disappointment though, as he could still hear the sound of rain above him. He scrambled out of his hiding place and looked out from under the bridge. Strange, he thought, he couldn't see any rain, yet still the noise continued. He pulled himself up onto the path and saw the culprit—not rain but dried up leaves being blown down a flight of stairs. Amazing, for he was convinced it was raining. Interesting how sounds can be so deceiving! He decided that was a good thing to remember—it might just save his life one day!

He went back to join the others who were all beginning to surface, although at the speed of teenagers on a school morning. Everyone was in dire need of food and water and, quite frankly, a lot more sleep; but they knew that wasn't possible, so they gathered their belongings and at a very steady pace headed for the port. They would find food and water there—it was full of restaurants offering plenty of choice, just as long as they could just keep themselves out of trouble.

As they neared their destination they split up, Nicodemus and Ophelia to get the water and the others to find some sustenance. "Over there," Nicodemus pointed towards an outside tap above a large, ground level, stone basin, used by humans for washing their feet after they'd been walking in the sand. "Quick, while the coast is clear." Without hesitation, Ophelia zoomed over to the tap. Fortunately it was dripping, as old taps often do, and she was able to hover conveniently close enough for Nicodemus to hold his canister under the drips and collect some water.

"That's two filled—just one more. Are you alright for a minute longer?" Nicodemus asked.

"Yes, fine, but be as fast as you can. I feel very exposed."

"Okay, I'll do my best."

Ophelia was on constant watch, looking out for any signs of danger when she caught sight of a human heading towards the tap.

"Quick, someone's coming! Let's just get out of here."

"Just putting the lid on."

Not quick enough though, and they were hit by a rapid blast of gushing water knocking Nicodemus flying, coughing and spluttering—and then sudden darkness and stillness. 'Am I dead?' he thought but was then splashed in the face by a wave. 'No, so where on earth am I, and where's Ophelia?'

"Phe, Phe, where are you?" He was desperately trying to work out what had happened to them. He was inside something long and thin and a fuzzy light was fighting its way through—but through what? He had no idea.

"I'm here, old friend. You can't get rid of me that quickly."

"I can't see you."

"Look up, I'm right above you."

"Thank goodness! Where are we? It's like we've been trapped inside a Viking long boat."

"I wish it was a boat but I'm afraid we're not that lucky. I think we're inside a pelican's beak. I didn't realise that he was behind us and the human I saw was coming to turn the tap on for him to have a drink. Trouble is, very soon he's going to want to swallow this water and us along with it!"

"Any bright ideas?"

"Actually, I do. I can sting him."

"Don't be ridiculous, you'll die."

"Nicodemus, how many times do I have to tell you I'm immortal?"

"This is not the time for light-hearted jokes, Ophelia. If you sting him you'll die."

"Shame on you, don't you know anything about me? I don't die when I use my sting! That's my cousin, the honey bee."

"Well, quit wasting time then and get on and sting this pelican so we can get the hell out of here! I can't tread water forever, you know, and I'm getting rather sick of the sight of it, to be perfectly honest."

He had hardly finished moaning when the lid of their capsule suddenly opened, letting in a furious beam of light, almost blinding them.

"Come on Nicodemus, let's go" Ophelia demanded.

"It's alright for you—I can't fly." Nicodemus was still complaining.

"Yes, and I'll drown if I get waterlogged."

"I thought you were immortal!"

"Nicodemus, you're incorrigible, I swear if I didn't think it would kill you I'd sting you too. Hold out your arms and grab the girth of my saddle." She flew down to him and as soon as she felt his weight beneath her she shot out of there. Any slower and they would have been lost forever as the mighty beak snapped shut right behind them.

"Oh God, I'm slipping! Quick, Phe, we need to land!" Nicodemus' hands were so wet and cold that he was having serious difficulty holding on. They had no time to get away so Ophelia just stopped where she was and let him slide onto the pelican's beak.

"Oh, it was you I have to thank for all that pain, was it?" The pelican said. As he spoke his beak went up and down, causing Nicodemus to roll about all over the place.

"Look, I'm really sorry about that but you were just about to swallow us," Nicodemus pointed out to him. "Do you think you could take us away from here? We're in a very vulnerable position, as you are such a big attraction to the tourists, someone is bound to see us." Nicodemus made sure he had a good grip before he finished speaking and this time when the pelican spoke he didn't move at all.

"Well, I guess as it was a life or death situation I forgive you, and if you sit tight I'll take you round to my secret hideout where I go to have some peace and quiet when I've had enough of the paparazzi."

"Thanks, we appreciate it," Nicodemus said. Ophelia arranged herself next to Nicodemus and was glad to be the passenger for once. The pelican took them through some narrow streets, not that that was a surprise, for all the streets are narrow in Chora and they all look the same, so it's very easy to get lost. (I spent ages trying to get back to my bus stop when I was there.) Gradually all the hustle and bustle of the port was behind them and they were in a tiny courtyard shielded by churches. The pelican stopped and rested his beak on the base of a monument so Nicodemus could shimmy off.

"Thanks a lot…" Nicodemus realised he did not know the pelican's name; he had been so keen to get away that he had forgotten all about formalities. "Sorry, I didn't ask you your name. I'm Nicodemus and this is Ophelia."

"I'm Pedros Junior—nice to meet you. Well, it wasn't to start with, but it is now." A funny little noise came from his throat, which I can only assume was his laugh.

"Junior?" Nicodemus questioned

"Yes, that's right. My predecessor was also called Pedros."

"Oh, right. This may sound a really stupid question, but why are you here? I didn't think pelicans lived in Greece. I wouldn't normally ask such silly questions and I'm sure if I asked Cadmus he would know the answer, but he's not here and I thought perhaps you wouldn't mind me asking." Nicodemus waffled to hide his embarrassment.

"I don't mind at all. Back in 1954 Pedros senior arrived. Legend has it that he was migrating when he was caught and injured in a storm. A local fisherman found him and nursed him back to health, but rather than continuing his migration he stayed here, and he became the island's official mascot until his death in 1986. The island was so saddened by his loss that Jackie Kennedy-Onassis donated Irene, a female pelican, and Hamburg Zoo donated me and they named me Pedros junior. It was just the two of us for a few years; then Nikolas, the youngest member of our trio, was injured in a storm during his migration. He too was nursed back to health, and the three of us have lived here ever since. Life's really good—we get lots of attention and fresh fish and when we've had enough we just come here for some shut-eye."

"That's fascinating, what a lovely story," Nicodemus said once Pedros had finished.

"What about you, what's your story?" Pedros asked in return.

"Nothing like your lovely story, I'm afraid. My daughter and niece have been kidnapped and are being held captive on the island of Delos. We have come to the port to catch a ride on one of the tourist boats. In fact, I think we better hurry or we might miss it and I can't bear the thought of my daughter spending another night imprisoned and afraid." Nicodemus rose to his feet. His clothes were still damp and he looked very dishevelled. He was past caring, for his only interest now was to rescue his family. "Thank you for your kindness, Pedros—it was a pleasure to meet you and hear your story." Nicodemus climbed aboard Ophelia who also said goodbye.

"You're very welcome. I wish you the best of luck on your journey and hope to meet you again some day, but perhaps under better circumstances!" Then Pedros nestled down, tucked his splendid pink and marbled grey beak under his wonderful feathered wing, slid his almost translucent eyelids over his friendly eyes and prepared himself for an enjoyable sleep in the warm midmorning sun.

“I do feel a bit like I’m stuck in an incubator.”

Chapter 17

Boat trip to Delos

Nicodemus met up with Ximena and Cadmus who had successfully gathered more food and Tyrone had thoughtfully collected some extra nectar, which Ophelia gladly accepted. She hadn't realised how hungry she had become until it was presented to her. They inconspicuously boarded the boat and found refuge under the tarpaulin that covered the bar stocks for the trip. They were all happy to sit in silence, eat, drink and contemplate until Ximena piped up, "Nicodemus, you know the well Vanessa mentioned?"

"Mmm," he confirmed

"Do you know where it is?"

"Not exactly, but I have a pretty good idea."

"That's a relief. One other thing…"

"Sounds ominous."

"Do you have a plan?"

"I do." Ophelia answered

"Great, let's hear it," Ximena said

"Well, my cousin has a colony on Delos and I was thinking, while you try and find Thaddea and Larissa, I'll go and ask them to come and help us; otherwise I struggle to see how we can possibly defeat Acantha's army. If we're honest with ourselves, we're completely outnumbered. I don't think we stand a chance without them."

"It is possible you know—think of David and Goliath, and Henry V in the battle of Agincourt—he was outnumbered 5000 to 25000 and he still won." Cadmus was the optimist, as always.

"Cadmus, Ophelia's right," Ximena said. "Surely we're better to come prepared than hope history will repeat itself in our favour?"

"Okay, we'll split up; then Phe and I will…"

"No, Nicodemus, I go alone. I will be much faster that way. Tyrone and Aldara are both bigger and stronger than I am and I'm sure they'll be able to take turns in carrying you."

"But Phe…"

"My mind's made up. I'll leave as soon as we land."

Silence swept over the group once more; then Nicodemus said, "Ophelia, may I speak with you alone?"

"Certainly, old friend, climb aboard. I'll take us somewhere quiet."

Carefully they crept out of the tarpaulin and Ophelia took to the air. They had not gone far when they were walloped by a rolled up magazine and sent flying across the bar until they dropped like a stone onto the work surface. Nicodemus was still alert enough to get out of sight and hid under Ophelia's fur. He heard a loud bang, peeped out and saw that they had been trapped underneath an upturned glass.

"Well, I found you somewhere quiet!" Ophelia remarked.

"Glad to see you haven't lost your sense of humour," Nicodemus said through all her fur, which was making him extremely hot but he couldn't risk being seen by the humans or they would be in even more trouble. (I'm not exactly sure how they could be in much more trouble, are you?) "Are you hurt?" he added.

"Don't think so—just a bit stunned and bruised. What about you?"

"The same really, only I do feel a bit like I'm stuck in an incubator with a fur blanket on. What do you think will get to me first—lack of oxygen or heat exhaustion?"

"Come now, Nicodemus, that's not the right attitude. What would Pia say if she were here now?"

"Well, she'd probably tell me to pull myself together."

"She might also mention that you smell bad and need a shave!" Ophelia giggled.

"Thanks for your support." Nicodemus tried to sound cross but it was a bit difficult when he knew she was right. He hadn't had a proper wash for days; all his clean clothes had either been lost or soaked and the ones he had on were caked in dirt and badly torn. His hair was just a big mat of tangles and he had old bits of food stuck between his teeth. If Pia had seen him like this, she would have definitely marched him off to the bathroom and told him not to return until he smelt of roses. How he missed her—he didn't think the hole in his heart would ever mend.

"Seriously now," Ophelia brought him back to his senses, "you know what she said to you from the fireplace. She warned you the journey would be fraught with danger. But she also told you that no matter what happened you must not give up. What else did she say?"

"That if I thought I couldn't go on anymore, that I should dig deep inside myself and use all my courage to go on." He was quiet for a moment, and then added, "She also said she'd be watching over me all the way."

"Right then, so we'll have no more talk of what will get to you first and instead think of a way to get out of this mess, so we can get to Thaddea before it's too late."

"Don't suppose you have a plan for that, do you?"

"As a matter of fact I do."

"Good, because I'm all out." Despite agreeing not to give up Nicodemus was feeling very despondent and not in the least bit courageous. He wondered how many more times he would find himself close to death before he got to see his daughter again.

"Well, I've been studying this glass and it looks as though it's marginally top heavy."

"Meaning?"

"Meaning, that if we can knock it off balance slightly it should fall over quiet easily."

"Lets do it." Nicodemus found new determination when he realised what Ophelia said was true and might actually work.

"On the count of three, we'll hit the side of the glass and keep hitting it until it falls. One two…"

"Wait, is that go on three or three then go?"

"*On* three—ready, one, two, three!" With tremendous force the pair of them rammed the side of the glass. It tilted slightly but then came back down to rest. The heat and lack of air was definitely getting to them but they weren't going to be beaten.

"Again!" Ophelia instructed and again they ploughed into the glass wall and again and again and again until it was really leaning like the Tower of Pisa; one last thump and it went crashing to the floor, sending shattered glass everywhere. The commotion caused enough of a distraction for Nicodemus and Ophelia to escape unnoticed.

Quickly they flew back to join the others in there safe hiding place. The pair of them collapsed in a heap. Nicodemus had just enough breath left to explain what had happened. Between them they decided to stay put until the boat docked at Delos.

...the room had filled with an acrid gritty powder
that was choking everyone.

Chapter 18

Escape Route

As they flew over the courtyard, Cleopatra and Lysandra saw Diomede sitting on the base of the torture trap with Ulysses by his side. Anxious to thank him and ask him where her father was being held, Cleopatra hurriedly flew down and landed next to him. He barely acknowledged her arrival and still did not look up even when she sat down next to him.

"Diomede, it was a brave thing to do, letting Lysandra free. You're not a coward, you..." Cleopatra was frustrated by the fact that Diomede would not look at her. "Diomede, please *look* at me—I don't want to talk to the top of your head." But when Diomede looked up she could see why his head had been hanging down. His right cheek was badly swollen and bruised and there was a deep gash just above his eye. Blood was trickling down his face and dropping into his lap.

"Who did this to you?" she gasped.

"Who do you think?" he replied, "This was punishment for setting Lysandra free. She said that Zeno would come to sort me out once and for all."

"Well, I'm not going to let him, come on, let's go now. We'll go to the dungeon and find father. He and Balthasa will help you escape, don't worry."

"I'm not going. I'll only get you and your father hurt. I'm going to stay here and face Zeno alone."

"Men!" She was exasperated. "Ulysses, you tell him," she ordered.

"Tried that. He's not listening to me either." And he just frowned and looked away.

"Well, I'm hardly going to be able to marry you if you're dead, am I?" Cleopatra announced, then promptly folded her arms and turned her back on him—not without giving Lysandra a quick wink first, however.

"Sorry, did you say what I thought you said?" Diomede sounded a bit uncertain.

"Of course I did, you great oaf. Now get up off your 'feeling sorry for yourself' backside and help me rescue my father, so he can give me away!"

For the first time in what felt like an eternity Diomede was filled with joy. He leapt up, swept Cleopatra off the floor and swung her round.

"Come on, we don't have time for this! Let's get going." Cleopatra was delighted but knew they had a lot of work to do if she stood any chance of getting married.

"You just try and stop me!" Diomede said as he jumped onto Ulysses.

"About time, too," said Ulysses with relief. Then the four of them set off in the direction of the dungeon.

Meanwhile, totally oblivious of her triumph, Stefan was worried sick about his daughter. He felt powerless, and for a king this was not a normal feeling—and he didn't care for it one bit, I hasten to add. He was not alone in his concerns. Larissa feared the worst about Vanessa as she had not been brought back to the dungeon, and Thaddea felt sure her father had suffered some terrible accident and she was to be left alone in the world, an orphan at 12-years-old. The only one not paralysed by their emotions was Balthasa; he knew it would be up to him to keep everyone calm and find a way of getting them out of there. While they had all been cooped up in the dingy dungeon he had carefully examined the structure of the walls and had noticed an area of damaged stone brickwork. He had come to the conclusion that this was due to a weakness in that section of the wall. Thaddea had just started to cry when he came up with an idea. He clicked his antlers together and said, "Okay everyone, I need your attention. I have worked out a way to get us out of here and I'm going to need your help."

They all stopped and stared at him.

"Go on," Stefan said, stroking his bushy white beard.

With everyone watching, Balthasa walked over to the wall. "I think this could be our way out," he said and he tapped one of the bricks. "If you look carefully, these bricks are damaged and I have a feeling that I can break through them using my antlers. It's going to create a lot of dust and rubble and I'm going to need you to keep the area clear so I can make a tunnel. Do you think you can do that?"

"Anything to get out of here," Larissa said.

"I'm with you," Stefan added.

"I'm not very strong," Thaddea admitted, "but I'll do my best."

"That's great, I'll get started." Balthasa started to pound the stone bricks like some powerful piece of machinery destroying a derelict building. Within seconds the room had filled with an acrid gritty powder that was choking everyone.

"Stop, Balthasa, stop!" Stefan yelled and then began coughing profusely. Balthasa ground to a halt and looked back around the room. As the dust began to settle he could see his companions bent double coughing and wheezing, their faces plastered in grime; there were streams of tears running down their faces like rivers in a muddy ravine.

"We're going to have to rethink, my friend. I only speak for myself but I know I won't last for long with this amount of dust getting into my lungs." Stefan was holding his chest and his face was contorting with the pain.

"Wait!" Thaddea burst out. "We can make masks, like mother used to wear when she was grinding the corn for flour."

"You're right! Masks, that's perfect." Then Larissa paused. "But how are we going to make them?"

"Stefan, may I have your cloak please?" Thaddea asked, nodding in corroboration, Stefan removed his cloak and weakly passed it to Thaddea.

"Stefan, are you sure you want to go through with this? You don't look well." Larissa was very concerned but he just raised his regal hand and gestured for them to continue. "How are we going to cut the cloth?" Larissa looked at Thaddea with a worried expression.

"Balthasa, if you wouldn't mind, could I use you for a minute?" For the first time since her imprisonment, Thaddea's young voice was filled with confidence.

"It would be a pleasure, my child." He had worked out what Thaddea was thinking and raised his antlers to a convenient height so she could use them to tear Stefan's cloak into long strips, ideal for wrapping around their faces. Then she walked over to Stefan, knelt down next to him and pulled a bottle of water out of her rucksack. She offered it to him and he received it gratefully. When he had finished she poured a small amount onto a piece of cloth and gently wiped his sorrowful eyes. They were sore from all the grit and filled with emptiness. She took another strip of material and poured water onto that one as well, but this was to help prevent the dust getting through. She carefully placed the mask around Stefan's face and tied it securely. She leant forward, kissed him tenderly on the cheek, and then whispered, "You should rest now. Don't worry, we'll get you out of here and find your daughter." Then she went and sat next to Larissa so they could sort out their own masks.

"Your mother would be very proud," Larissa said, affectionately rubbing Thaddea's back. "And we'll get you out of here safely, too, and when we do I shall be the first to tell Nicodemus about your unyielding bravery and compassion."

They used the remains of the cloth like a dustsheet and laid it on the ground next to the hole Balthasa had made. This time when Balthasa started they were ready and began to collect the crumbled stones in the sheet, when it was covered they dragged it across the floor and heaved it over so the rubble fell off into a heap in the corner, then they went back for another load.

Things were going well for the in flight rescuers too - "How long until we reach the well?" Cleopatra asked Diomede as they sped through the air.

"Not long now and you'll be back with your father."

"I shouldn't count on it."

Diomede spun round. "You!" Right on their tail was Zeno and a troop of locusts. "You're the errand boy now, are you? Let's face it, once she's disposed of me you'll be the only one left foolish enough to believe in her. She'll turn on you too, you know. She doesn't care about anyone apart from herself."

"Gallant words from someone facing death, how noble," Zeno scoffed. "Take them," he said, and waved the troop forward who swarmed downwards at such speed that the noise was like that of an aeroplane's engine vibrating. As Diomede looked down he saw a huge net spread out below him. Before he had a chance to think of how he could escape, the locusts flew straight up, catching him and Cleopatra on the way. They were crushed both physically and emotionally. There was little hope of them rescuing Stefan now. In fact, their chances of surviving at all were looking pretty slim.

“Quick, they’re gaining on us!”

Chapter 19

Locusts and Lions

When the boat had docked and all the tourists disembarked, the travellers crept out from under the safety of the tarpaulin. As agreed, Ophelia left in search of her cousin's colony, leaving Aldara to carry Cadmus, Nicodemus and one of the saddlebags.

Nicodemus was pretty sure the well that Vanessa spoke of was in the region of the Avenue of the Lions and the sacred lake, although it was a long time since he had been there and he wasn't certain. He decided that as he had no other way of finding out what was where, they should start looking. They knew they had to fly quite low because the well was at ground level, but that would make things more risky due to the large number of tourists circulating the site. Mind you, Cadmus was thrilled at the prospect of getting up close to all the ruins—he was in his element telling them what each one was as they flew past; they weren't so thrilled, however, and kept telling him to be quiet.

"Hang on Aldara, there's a butterfly down there—let's go and ask her if she knows where the well is," Nicodemus suggested. He told Ximena what he was going to do and they arranged to meet at the lions after she had looked around some other places.

"Ready?" Aldara asked and when Nicodemus agreed she flew down towards a magnificent yellow and black boldly striped butterfly merrily enjoying some lunch from one of the very few flowers found on Delos.

"Excuse me," Nicodemus began, "I was wondering if you could tell me where I might find the island's well."

"I know nothing, I'm from Barcelona!" was the extent of the reply.

"Sorry to have bothered you," Nicodemus sighed and Aldara took off again.

"That was a Spanish Swallowtail," Cadmus boasted, "and a mighty fine specimen I must say."

"Well, it would have been nice if you'd bothered to mention that before we wasted valuable time and energy."

"Sorry, I thought I'd get told off for boring you with trivia when you were doing something important," he whined

"I think you should let me be the judge of that in future, okay?"

"Okay," he conceded.

They were back on course for the lions when Nicodemus realised that the tourists were all running away from them. Well, he knew it couldn't have been from them, so he turned to see what had scared them.

"Oh God, it's Zeno and his army, Aldara—fly like the wind!"

Aldara set off at full speed but the added weight of Nicodemus meant she began to tire very quickly.

"Nicodemus, I can't outrun them for long—what shall we do?" She was panicking and Nicodemus could hear it in her voice.

"Can you get to the lions?"

"I think so, then what?"

"We can hide up inside the jaw of one of them until we think of what to do."

"Quick, they're gaining on us!" Cadmus shouted. "Oh no, Ximena and Tyrone are behind us! We'll have to go back and help them."

"NO!" Nicodemus bellowed. He felt awful but he knew that if they went back they might all be killed.

"Oh God, I can't look!" Cadmus buried his head in his arm just as Zeno's army caught up with Ximena.

Nicodemus, on the other hand, did look and witnessed a horrendous battle as Tyrone did his best to use his mighty strength to hold off the locusts while Ximena fought courageously—but unfortunately to no avail, and when a group of locusts joined forces and smashed into them, Tyrone was tipped upside down. He couldn't right himself and Ximena lost her grip. Both of them fell from view and Nicodemus could only pray that because they had been flying low that they would have survived.

Having been occupied with Ximena and Tyrone, the locusts had lost sight of Nicodemus and that had given them enough time to hide inside one of the lions. Cadmus thought it resembled a Brontosaurus and not a lion, but thought now was probably not the time to broach the subject. "I hope Ximena's okay," he said instead.

"I'm sure she is," Nicodemus said hopefully. "She's pretty tough, you know. It won't be long before Zeno works out where we are and I've got no idea how we're going to get out of this." He glanced around in a last ditch effort for some inspiration when in the distance he spotted smoke. It must have been some dried grass on fire. It is quite a regular occurrence in Greece, although not usually so late in the season. He scrambled about in his pocket and to his relief felt a box of matches. He knew he'd had some for their camp fires—he just hadn't been sure they would still be in his pocket after all that had happened.

"I've got it," he said excitedly, and together the three of them hatched a plan.

They checked the coast was clear and Aldara swiftly flew down to the ground and dropped off Nicodemus and the supplies; then she and Cadmus headed towards Zeno who had been circling the area, trying to find them.

Nicodemus set to work. He didn't have much time and would have to run, not something he aspired to do. They had decided to set a trap, seeing the smoke had given Nicodemus the idea of lighting a fire and tricking the locusts into chasing Aldara and being caught in the flames. The initial problem was that they were not likely to follow her if they saw the flames, but then Nicodemus remembered his faithful whisky that he carried in the lovely hip flask that Pia had given him—purely for medicinal purposes, you understand. He knew that alcohol produced a flame that was almost invisible to the eye and it wasn't until other things around it caught fire that you could actually see the flames. So that was what he had to do—pour the whisky over the ground set light to it, and then Aldara was to fly really low over the top of it with the army behind her and hope that the grass had been dried up enough by the sun to catch light easily and engulf the locusts, giving Aldara just enough time to escape out the other side.

All was going according to plan. Nicodemus had mapped out a large area with whisky, although he was now completely out of breath and dripping in sweat. He wasn't used to having to exert so much energy. Flying was definitely his preferred option. It made him think of Ophelia, and he wished she would return soon, not only because he was totally exhausted but also, hopefully, because she would have help with her.

Now for the moment of truth! He crouched down, took out the box of matches and drew one from the box and went to light it. His heart froze, for the match just crumpled in his hand. It had been ruined from getting wet. He couldn't believe it! He could see Aldara in the distance—she had already got the attention of Zeno and was on her way back. Hurriedly, he pulled out another match and the same happened. In his haste to get a third, he pulled the box right open and all the matches scattered over the ground, some of them falling in the whisky, rendering themselves completely useless—assuming they hadn't already been so. He scrabbled about, picked up a match, struck it on the box, and—it lit! "Thank God!" he breathed, but as he leant forward to light the ground a huge bead of sweat dropped from his forehead and landed directly on the flame, extinguishing it instantly. Aldara was speeding towards him with the army in hot pursuit so he picked up the matchbox and frantically looked inside one more time. To his utter relief he saw one solitary match! He clasped it between his finger and thumb and struck it against the side of the box. "Come on!" he begged. Finally, a flame! Without hesitation he ran it along the whisky trail and as he glanced back he could just see a heat haze, the sort you get from tarmac on a hot summer's day. Aldara was nearly upon him and he hadn't left himself much time to get out of the way. He launched himself under the nearest rock just as Aldara flew overhead.

"I hope Nicodemus was right about this," Cadmus said to Aldara as they approached the purple haze of burning whisky.

"You're not doubting my speed, are you?"

"It's not yours I'm worried about, it's the bunch of half starved locusts that clearly want to have us for their next meal that are bothering me."

"Hang on, young man, we are just shifting up a gear. Warp speed sound good to you?"

"Beam me up, Scottie!"

Just as they entered the alcoholic vapour the grass went up in a mass of angry flames. The heat was instant and unbearable. Cadmus' eyes were stinging and his throat felt like sandpaper. The locusts were right behind them and caught in the inferno just as planned.

"Oh God, Aldara, can you get us out of here?" Cadmus choked on the fumes.

"I'm faster than they are, have faith. Keep your head down and breathe through your nose." She may have sounded confident but she was suffering terribly; she could feel her wings being singed by the flames and she was having trouble keeping them beating separately as they were sticking to one another. She just kept telling herself that she was going to make it and used all her strength to fight her way through the blaze.

"We made it!" Cadmus said as he wiped his eyes. He could smell the burnt hair from his eyebrows and nose; some of his skin had blistered from the heat and his once crisp white shirt was black from the smoke, but considering what had happened to the locusts he wasn't doing too badly. "Aldara, speak to me! Are you okay?"

"Only just. I need to land quickly before I crash." She sounded dreadful.

"How about over there?" he pointed towards a lone palm tree which looked like it had once had pride of place in a splendid lake but was now just surrounded by grass and a low dilapidated stone wall. As they neared the wall they saw Nicodemus, who was wandering around aimlessly.

"We're heading for the tree," Cadmus rasped, his throat still very painful from all the smoke inhalation. Aldara hovered painfully while they spoke.

"I must find Ximena," he shouted back.

"Aldara's injured but I'll help."

"No, you stay with her—she needs you. When I find Ximena I'll bring her to the tree."

"Did we get all the locusts?" Cadmus asked hopefully.

"All but Zeno and Theron, I saw him pull up at the last moment. He's disappeared now—probably gone to tell Acantha."

"It was a good plan, Nicodemus. We couldn't have beaten them any other way. Ophelia will be impressed."

"Cadmus, please." Aldara was listing.

"We have to go, good luck Nicodemus."

"Take care of Aldara." Nicodemus went back to his searching while his friends flew to the safety of the tree.

“You mustn’t worry about her, that’s Hermione.”

Chapter 20

March of the Ants

Nicodemus was beginning to feel very alone and apprehensive. He knew he had to find Ximena. She could be lying somewhere badly injured and vulnerable. He was certain Tyrone would protect her, but what if he were hurt too? It was like looking for a needle in a haystack (Not that I've ever tried, but so I hear); it was near on impossible, for being on foot was so laborious it was taking him ages just to cover the smallest area, and he hadn't eaten for ages and was absolutely starving; at least, he was getting thinner, but that really wasn't much compensation for everything that had happened.

He sat down on a pebble and gave a huge sigh and his tummy rumbled by way of a reply. Suddenly the ground started to shake. Soon it became so fierce that he was nearly bounced off his seat! He dreaded to think what horror might be heading his way, but his lethargy stopped him from getting up and running. He had resigned himself to imminent death—and then he was amazed to hear…

"Left, left, left right left. Left, left, left right left. I don't know but I've been told…"

"Sergeant Briggs is very old!"

Then there was an almighty crunch as the leader stopped dead in his tracks and the procession all marched into one another.

"And who may I ask, are *you*?" spoke a very austere and pompous soldier ant.

"Hello there, I'm Nicodemus—and who are you?"

"I'm asking the questions around here! Now what is the purpose of your visit to our Island? You do realise you are trespassing, don't you?"

"Sorry sir, no, I didn't" Nicodemus thought it best to go along with the façade. "I was here searching for my daughter when we were ambushed by an army of locusts and my niece was knocked out of the sky. I have been trying to find her ever since."

"And the locusts?"

"We set a trap and baked them in a fire." Nicodemus wasn't too sure how well that would be received but was relieved by the reply:

"Jolly good! Damned brutes have polished off most of our vegetation. What does this niece of yours look like then?"

"Um, well, she is about the same size as me with short blonde hair and has a Cardinal Beetle with her."

"Excuse me, sir." One of the ants had stepped out of line. (Not sure whether that was brave or stupid.)

"Yes boy, come on, speak up! Important business this, you know; missing person's involved here—no time for stammering."

"Well sir, my brother is in Sergeant Briggs' division and after their march this morning he told me that he had seen someone fitting that description not far from here." The smaller ant stepped backwards in anticipation of the sergeant's response but fortunately the information had been well received.

"Good work boy! You and the others go in front and see what you can find. Oh, and your brother hasn't told Sergeant Briggs what we sing, has he?" The question was put forward with some trepidation.

"No sir, definitely not, sir."

"Good! Well, on your way then! Up two, up two." Then the ant turned back to Nicodemus. "My boys will find your niece and bring her back to you, as a thank you for ridding us of those blasted locusts."

"Thank you so much. That's very kind."

"Think nothing of it!" Then the ant saluted and began the march once again.

Nicodemus was sitting quietly contemplating how he was going to find Thaddea when the ant procession returned and with them Ximena and Tyrone; he watched in amazement as the ant convoy turned itself into a conveyor belt and with total ease carried Ximena to the front, followed shortly afterwards by Tyrone and the Chief ant.

"Job done, Nicodemus—one niece returned safe and sound! Anything else we can do for you, old chap?"

"Watch out!" Ximena screamed as she saw a lizard, that, as we already know, not only eats ants but Kintfoly people as well.

"You mustn't worry about her. That's Hermione—she's vegetarian, something to do with her name meaning 'of the earth'; says she won't eat anything unless it has grown out of the earth. Fruit loop, if you ask me, but it's quite handy, really—at least she doesn't eat us."

Now that Nicodemus was happy because he wasn't just about to become lizard lunch, he took a minute to admire her. Although her body was quite a dull grey green colour, her head was a fiery mix of sunset orange and banana yellow. She had enormous and powerful hind legs and a surprisingly fat tail. "Phew, that's a relief!" he eventually answered. "I don't think there is anything else you can do, although, can you just excuse me for a minute?" And Nicodemus turned to Ximena who had come and sat next to him. "What's happened to Tyrone? Can he fly?"

"No, he can't. His shell cracked when we fell and he can't open his wing properly."

"Oh dear! Excuse me sir, you couldn't help us for a little while longer, could you? It's just that I need to get Tyrone to the palm tree for safety and I don't think I can manage by myself."

"I tell you what, I have a better idea—Hermione!" The ant called over to the lizard, who casually sauntered over and lowered her head right down to take a better look.

"Afternoon sir, pleasure to see you, how's the family?" she asked the ant pleasantly.

"Good, thank you! I wonder if you would be kind enough to help these poor people? They are having a bit of a rough time of it and need to get over to the palm tree. Do you think you could oblige?"

"It would be a pleasure—anything to help a friend in need." She stood perfectly still so the ants carrying Tyrone could march up her scaly side and then they placed him gently on her back.

"You next, missy," Chief ant said to Ximena, but as she rose to her feet she suddenly keeled over. Nicodemus jumped up and caught her. When he had laid her down he saw blood all across his shirt. He tilted her head slightly to find a deep wound at the base of her skull. There was a lot of congealed blood in her hair and fresh blood was still weeping from the cut. He hadn't seen it before because she had either been facing him or been sitting next to him. He tore off the bottom of his shirt and noticed that his once very flabby overhang was beginning to diminish. At least something was going right! He wrapped the material around Ximena's head and with the help of the ants got her and himself up onto Hermione's back.

Hermione got them to the palm tree as fast as she could, but before they'd even stopped Nicodemus was shouting, "Cadmus, come quickly, I need your help!" By the time they had stopped Cadmus was at the base of the tree waiting.

"Crikey, what's happened to them both?"

"Well, Tyrone's not too bad; his shell is cracked and he can't fly, but other than that he seems okay. However, it's Ximena—she has a nasty cut on the back of her head and she's fainted."

"Okay, let's get them out of the sun and find somewhere comfortable for them to recuperate." Hermione helped the best she could by getting right up close to the tree so they could pull Tyrone and Ximena into one of the holes in the trunk. I think they were originally made by birds for nesting, but they turned out to be an ideal hospital room for everyone. Cadmus stayed inside while Nicodemus went back out to speak to Hermione.

"I couldn't ask you one more favour, could I?"

"But of course."

“What power do I have to defeat these slithering serpents?”

Chapter 21

Snake Charmer

Hermione had kindly agreed to take Nicodemus to the well. She managed to get him quite close but there were so many pesky tourists chasing after her, pointing and taking pictures that she had to bail out, leaving him with a short walk and the promise that if he ever needed her again he should just whistle. He didn't mind the walk and Hermione had been a tremendous help, and it had given him a chance to rest and recharge his batteries, so to speak.

As he approached the entrance to the well he could see some movement across the circular stone ledge that surrounded it. He had prepared himself for something like this, knowing full well that Acantha would have protected her dungeon. But snakes! Why did it have to be snakes! He hated them. But he didn't have the time to worry about that now. He had to work out how he could get past them and find Thaddea. He stopped where he was for a moment. 'Back to David and Goliath again,' he thought. "What power do I have that can defeat these slithering serpents?" he asked himself, not really expecting a sensible answer, but to his astonishment he got one. "I know, I could sing and send them to sleep. That way I can creep past them and get inside the well."

With a solution to his dilemma all he needed now was something to make his very own tannoy system. Nicodemus knew that snakes didn't have external ears but instead hear by sensing vibrations, so he needed to find a way of creating the right sound to produce the soporific effect he required. To his delight he noticed a ring pull from a can dropped by a tourist! It would be perfect for reverberating sound. He took his rope from the saddlebag that he now had strapped to his back. He was glad he had been sensible enough to bring it with him. He crept over to the can, tied the rope through the finger hole and heaved it up onto the ledge; it banged against a flint but the noise didn't attract the snake's attention. Nicodemus wiped his brow and took a swig of water from his canister. It was warm and not in the least bit refreshing, but nonetheless was enough to moisten his vocal chords ready for singing. He was able to get quite close to the snakes. It was to his advantage that they don't see well and as long as he didn't make any sudden movements he should be okay.

He pursed his lips and then broke into song. He had carefully positioned the ring pull so it deflected the sounds straight towards the snakes' ears. Then it dawned on him, how on earth was he going to know if his plan had worked when he remembered snakes do not have moveable eyelids; they don't blink and they certainly don't shut their eyes to go to sleep. Well, there was nothing else for it besides assuming that they were in an hypnotic state and after a couple of minutes singing he skilfully untied the rope and wedged the end of it under a rock so he could abseil down the wall of the well and find the door to the dungeon.

As he lowered himself down, he felt the rock moving. He prayed it would hold him long enough to find the door, just as if his prayers had been answered he instantly saw it! He took a firm grip on the rope and swung towards the door, snatching at its hinges. Just then, the rock tipped up, releasing the rope and Nicodemus hit the ground with a wallop, fortunately his excess padding stopped him from being badly hurt. The rope came whirling over the edge and landed all coiled up on the steps next to him, that had apparently appeared out of nowhere. It was then he realised that there had been no need for all those heroics, as a perfect spiral staircase led all the way up to the top of the well. 'Typical!' he thought.

He was in the process of deciding how he was going to knock the door down when his attention was drawn to a clanking sound above his head. He looked up to see the best thing he'd seen all day—the keys! They were swaying gently in the breeze that had been caused by the rope falling! He reached up and took them down. The lock was a bit stiff but with a bit of jiggling he was able to dislodge it and open the door. It was difficult to make out what was going on as the room was filled with dust and there was an awful lot of noise.

"Thaddea, Thaddea, are you in here?" he called. He heard nothing in return so he waded his way through the smog in the direction of the noise. Again he shouted, "Thaddea! Are you in here?"

"Father! Is that you?" The words were sweet music to his ears, a voice he feared he would never hear again, and his daughter appeared from the curtain of dust. He draped his arms around her and the hole in his heart was miraculously filled with joy. The trauma and trepidation of his journey were finally being rewarded and his loneliness was no more.

"I thought I'd never find you!" he said at last.

"I knew you'd come," she said as she burrowed even deeper into his chest.

"Where's all this dust coming from?"

"That's Balthasa—he's digging us a way out."

"Who's Balthasa?"

"King Stefan's Stag beetle."

Nicodemus was just about to ask who he was as well, when he realised that Larissa was standing in front of him. His sadness returned when he was cruelly reminded that Larissa's beautiful butterfly, Vanessa, had died and he would have to be the one to give her the news.

Larissa could see in Nicodemus' face that all was not good. "Vanessa didn't make it, did she?" she asked woefully.

"I'm sorry my love," he said, reaching out an arm to comfort her. "I wouldn't have found you without her help, you know. She was courageous right up to the end and the last thing she said was, 'tell Larissa I love her'."

Hearing those words were too much for Larissa and the tears flowed heavily. In between sobs she asked, "Why isn't Ximena with you? Please don't tell me she's dead too."

"No, but she's badly injured and she urgently needs your help."

Nicodemus was not sure how to handle this delicate situation. He knew she would need to grieve but if they didn't get out of there soon there would be a whole lot more to worry about. Then Balthasa came to his rescue.

"I'm through!" he yelled, and then saw Nicodemus. "Who are you?" he asked.

"This is my father! He's come to rescue us," Thaddea said proudly.

"Any chance we can get out the way you came in?" Although the tunnel was finished it was dangerous and Balthasa hoped there would be an easier way.

"Not if those snakes wake up there isn't," Nicodemus replied.

"Okay, we'll have to take our chances with the tunnel then. Let's hurry before anyone comes."

Larissa shook her head, dried her eyes on her sleeve, took a deep breath and followed Balthasa. Nicodemus and Thaddea brought up the rear. Thaddea was still tightly gripping Nicodemus' arm.

"Can you help Stefan?" Balthasa asked Nicodemus. "I need to stay at the front to clear the way in case the earth moves. I don't think he'll make it otherwise."

"No problem, Thaddea darling. I need you to let go just for a minute so I can help Stefan."

"It's okay father, I'll help too." They took an arm each and helped Stefan to his feet.

"I don't suppose you have news of my daughter, Cleopatra, do you?" Stefan asked once he was stable.

"I'm afraid not. I haven't been to the kingdom yet but I should think that's where Acantha's hiding the Beryl stone; so I shall be going there next."

"I'll join you," Stefan croaked.

"I think not, dear king," Balthasa said firmly. "It is my job to keep you safe, and taking you to face Acantha would be like signing your death warrant."

"Balthasa's right. You are in no fit state to take on Acantha. I have a friend who will take you, Larissa and Thaddea to safety."

"I'm not going anywhere without you," Thaddea interrupted.

"Darling, please."

"I mean it, father. I have already lost my mother—I'm not losing you too."

"If you insist, but we'll have to find someone for you to ride—and me, for that matter," Nicodemus realised.

"Balthasa at your service," he said, bowing his head.

"That's settled then—now let's get going."

"Who is this friend you speak of?" Stefan asked as they entered the tunnel.

"You'll see," Nicodemus said, smiling. He didn't think now was quite the right time to try and explain Hermione.

… like a demon unleashed, chased after Acantha.

Chapter 22

Argus Attacks

After a dirty and claustrophobic struggle through the tunnel they all arrived safely at the surface, fortunately far enough away from the snakes to go unnoticed. As they patted down their clothing and shook the mud from their hair, Nicodemus let rip an ear-piercing whistle.

"Whoa! You could have warned me," Larissa said. "What did you do that for anyway?"

"Larissa, meet Hermione."

And trotting across the remains of a mosaic floor ran his favourite lizard.

"You must be joking!" Larissa muttered under her breath.

"No, he's not," Balthasa confirmed. "This is Hermione, friend to all insects on Delos and, of course, the Kintfoly people."

"Good afternoon your majesty, it would appear you've had better days," Hermione said to Stefan with genuine concern.

"Indeed I have, my scaly friend. Do you think you would be kind enough to take me to join Nicodemus' companions?"

"It would be my pleasure. Are you travelling alone or is anyone else taking first class today?"

Nicodemus stepped forward. "If it's not too much trouble, can you take Larissa too?"

"No trouble at all! All aboard, no in-flight meal today, I'm afraid, but I think there are refreshments on arrival." Once Larissa and Stefan were settled Hermione looked at Nicodemus and said, "Take care of yourself now and don't worry about your friends—they are in good hands." Then she scurried out of sight, leaving Nicodemus to find someone for Thaddea to ride on. It wasn't long before he found a group of Fire Flies bustling about amongst some pretty little flowers. He wasn't sure what they were but didn't doubt Cadmus would have known. He approached with caution, then asked,

"Excuse me, I'm sorry to interrupt. You all look very busy but we have a small emergency and are in dire need of a flying angel to come to our aid."

"If it's a flying angel you need, then I'm your girl." It was the tiniest member of the group who spoke up. She was exquisite to look at, her features so young and delicate, yet she carried upon her back a shell of defiance to any predator; it was made from blushing red and ink-black markings that formed a face like that seen on the top of a totem pole. She was designed this way so she looked much bigger than she really was to anyone flying overhead who might be feeling a bit peckish.

"Why, thank you, little one. How kind if you to offer." She was so tiny, in fact, that Nicodemus felt quite big for once. It didn't matter though because her job would be to escort Thaddea to the Kingdom and as Thaddea was tiny, too, they were perfectly matched. Nicodemus continued, "I have some very precious cargo that needs a fearless companion. Do you think you could handle the job?"

"You can count on me, sir. My name is Delia, meaning 'one who came from Delos' and there's nothing I wouldn't do for its protection."

"You are truly a bold little thing, aren't you? Well I, Nicodemus of Beryllos, accept your generous offer and welcome you to our family. This is Thaddea, my daughter." Who dutifully stepped forward to make herself known and beamed at Delia and tickled her under the chin. "And this magnificent beast is Balthasa, the king's right-hand man." Balthasa bowed and said,

"May the Lord protect the king."

"I do hope so," Nicodemus said.

"No, I mean, that's what my name means—may the Lord protect the king."

"Nonetheless I still hope he does!" Nicodemus insisted. "Well, now we have the introductions over and done with we must leave; we still have to find Stefan's daughter and the Beryl Stone."

"Tally ho!" Balthasa yelled as he took off. 'Must be down to his English ancestry', Nicodemus thought, knowing full well that was not the sort of expression a Greek would use.

Fortunately it was not a long ride to the castle as the day had once again become swelteringly hot and Nicodemus was so debilitated that he was finding it hard to remain focused.

"Father, we're here," Thaddea said as they flew over the wall into the castle grounds.

"Okay, my love. Balthasa, do you have any idea where we might find Cleopatra?" Nicodemus enquired.

"It would be my guess that she's taken refuge in the North Tower."

"Let's look there..." But before he could finish they were hit by a surly,

"Not so fast!" It was Acantha accompanied, as always, by Danae and Perseus, her loathsome hornets. "Your pitiful charade ends here, Nicodemus! Never in a million years will you beat me."

Nicodemus was scanning his brain with the slightest glimmer of hope that yet another great plan would manifest itself when he felt a sudden chill in the air. He noticed Acantha had felt it too because they both turned round at the same time to be confronted by what could only be described as 'Argus', the Greek Giant with 100 eyes. However, this was no man but instead a hostile swarm of Honey Bees in the formation of a giant and, with five eyes each, they certainly gave a good impression of Argus. Nicodemus' glimmer of hope had arrived. Ophelia had finally returned with her cousin and his colony and for once it was Acantha who was outnumbered. She was preparing her escape when the giant broke formation and like a demon unleashed, chased after Acantha. They caught hold of Danae, ripped her from the chains of the chariot, and engulfed her in a violent and dangerous pulsating ball.

"Oh my God, what are they doing!" Thaddea shrieked.

"That, my dear, is the ball of death," Nicodemus replied with very little sympathy. "Our native Honey Bees surround the hornet and then net themselves so tightly together that the hornet's abdomen is crushed and it can't breathe so it suffocates."

"That's horrible!" Thaddea replied.

"The Asian bees make their ball so hot that they actually bake the hornet to death," Balthasa joined in for some additional gruesome effect.

The tone changed abruptly when, from out of nowhere, Ophelia appeared.

"That's for Vanessa!" she screamed at Perseus, who was in shock from witnessing the death of his mother. "And you're next!"

"Wrong again, twinkle toes," Acantha cried as she freed Perseus from his chains, leapt on his back and fled, shouting behind her: "And don't think you've got rid of me that easily—I'll be back!"

And before Nicodemus could do so much as blink she had vanished into thin air. "That just leaves Zeno and Diomede," he thought out loud.

"I expect they disappeared when they saw Argus," Ophelia declared.

"Great plan, Phe, well done," said Nicodemus. "Oh, and it's nice to see you."

"Nice to be seen, big guy, although not as big as you were, I see." She chuckled.

"I don't think we should worry about Zeno and Diomede unless we have to," Balthasa urged, "but I do think we should continue our search for Cleopatra as quickly as possible."

"We're right behind you," Nicodemus said and without the faintest idea about what they were letting themselves in for, they flew towards the North Tower.

… he had been frozen stiff by a miniature Dactyl.

Chapter 23

The Final Curtain

Once the North Tower was in sight, Balthasa could see Cleopatra's window was slightly ajar.

"Clever girl," he said, "must have known we'd come for her." And he slowed down for the others to catch up with him. He was faster than them because he wasn't carrying anyone now Ophelia was back and Nicodemus had joined her.

"That's Cleopatra's window. I expect she's left it open for us but proceed with caution. It's just as likely to be one of Acantha's traps."

They listened intently, entered vigilantly and landed soundlessly. The room was immaculate but there was no sign of Cleopatra or Lysandra. Nevertheless, they still examined the room rigorously; besides, Cleopatra could have stowed herself away in the old wooden blanket chest or under the huge four-poster bed. Perhaps she had draped the great linen curtains over her innocent body. Unfortunately this was not the case and the search had to continue.

Now all were on foot because flying was not possible. They crept out of the door and along the landing. Ophelia was winding her way down the spiral staircase when she heard a disturbance behind her. Impulsively she turned to see what was causing it, but she slipped on the polished steps, lost her balance and fell headlong down the stairs, ending up in a motionless, deathly silent bundle.

Nicodemus' automatic reaction would have been to run to her; however, as he had been frozen stiff by a miniature Dactyl (presumably created by the larger wizard Dactyls for just this kind of job) who had been hiding inside a classic grandfather clock, this was going to make running a bit difficult. She had squeezed herself inside, stopped the pendulum in mid-swing and waited patiently for her victim to arrive. He tried to flex his fingers but nothing happened, not even when he attempted to wriggle his toes. The only moveable parts left were his eyes that were darting about madly, scrutinizing everything in their path, looking for the culprit. It was Thaddea who came to his rescue: she had been following a short distance behind him when the spell was cast and the door of the clock being slowly teased open caught the attention of her eager young eyes. She silently removed her rucksack from her back and rummaged about amongst the contents until she found what she was looking for. Without considering the consequences, she jumped forward, flung open the door of the clock and shone her mirror right into the face of the Dactyl. The creatures' squeals could be heard right across the kingdom and were so shrill that the beautiful crystal vase standing on a nearby mantelpiece shattered into a hundred tiny pieces. Thaddea kept pointing the mirror even though the sound was searing through her like a hot poker; her perseverance paid off and the Dactyl disappeared in a puff of smoke. As soon as it had gone the spell was released and Nicodemus ran over to her,

"You clever girl! How did you know that would work?"

"Well, I didn't really. It's just that I'd heard fairies can't stand to see their reflection."

"Good work! We're all going to have to keep on our toes—there's bound to be more where she came from. Now, we must get to Ophelia—she's not moving." But before he could make it down the stairs, his concerns were realised when, dropping from the ceiling like SAS soldiers, were more Dactyls who were hanging from twisted vines that had sprung up from nowhere. Nicodemus unclipped his iron bracelet and thrust it in the face of one of the Dactyls, who was particularly ugly—not like Celosia, he thought, although her beauty was most certainly only skin deep. (Isn't it amazing how appearances can be very deceiving!)

"You idiot!" she cackled. "Don't you know anything about fairy magic? We Dactyls are smiths and work with Iron so it cannot harm us, not like those flimsy Sylvans—one ounce of metal and they're all in a fluster."

"Run!" Nicodemus shouted, but he had hardly gone a foot when he, Balthasa and Thaddea were surrounded. Quickly, Thaddea grabbed her mirror once more, but to her horror saw that it too had shattered from the first Dactyl's screams. It was Nicodemus who remembered something this time and said, "On the count of three, run! One, two…"

"Is that on three or…" Thaddea started to ask but then…

"*Three*!" and Nicodemus had taken some torn gardening gloves from his back pocket and hurled them into the middle of the fairy ring. Instantly the fairies dispersed and at the same time the terrified trio ran—all in the same direction, thank goodness.

"This way!" Balthasa yelled and he took them through a narrow corridor lined from floor to ceiling with books. Uncharacteristically, he started ripping at the books with his antlers.

"Balthasa, what in God's name are you doing?" Nicodemus asked, totally bemused and a little anxious, as he was sure the fairies would have reformed and be after them already.

"Quickly, behind one of these books is a lever! It will take us to a secret room." They all scrabbled about wildly tearing the books from the shelves. Nicodemus felt dreadful desecrating such fine work but he knew he had no choice if he wanted to survive.

"I've got it!" Thaddea said, and yanked the handle down. Unbelievably the floor they were standing on began to move and the entire bookshelf began to rotate until it came to a halt on the other side of the wall.

"No time to lose! We must wedge the lever or they'll be right in behind us."

Nicodemus glanced helplessly around the room. There were oil portraits of previous royalty, and an elegant standing lamp that was no good for wedging the door with, he thought. Then he noticed how dark it was: there were no windows (that could prove to be a problem). As his eyes wandered around the room he also noticed a delicate screen covered in rich coloured embroidery that had been used by ladies to change behind, he assumed, and then…

"Will this do?" came a hand reaching out from behind the screen, holding a large metal candlestick.

"Perfect, thanks," Nicodemus said, stretching over to it. Then realising what was happening, he nearly jumped out of his skin.

Out from behind the screen calmly stepped Cleopatra. "Sorry to startle you," she said and was about to introduce herself when Balthasa exclaimed,

"Cleopatra! You're alive, thank God!"

"Where's father?" she asked

"Don't worry, he's fine and far from here. How do we get out of here, and how did you get in?" Balthasa questioned.

"We'd been caught by Zeno and locked in the round room. He was keeping watch until Acantha summoned him and then we were left alone. It didn't take long for us to break out and then we needed to find somewhere to hide. I knew this room existed because as a child I'd discovered it by accident when I'd been looking through some of the books in the corridor. I'm afraid the only way out is the way you came in."

"Oh, great! What smart Alec invented a secret room with only one exit?" said Balthasa with a rather disheartened sigh. "And who's *we*? Do you have Lysandra hiding here too?"

"Yes, and don't panic; but Diomede is with me, too."

"What! Are you mad?" Nicodemus was furious. "You'll get us all killed."

Cleopatra did not need to answer because from out of an old battered wardrobe stepped Diomede and Ulysses, who looked decidedly unimpressed at having been squashed inside somewhere that had quite clearly not been designed for hiding in.

"Hello, everyone, please don't be alarmed, I mean you no harm..." he started but before he could finish, Thaddea said,

"What happened to your face?"

"My mother attacked me for freeing Lysandra. She was going to let Theron and the other locusts kill her, so I had to do something."

"Your own *mother* did this to you? No wonder you want to be our friend! You can stay with us—can't he, father?" Thaddea beseeched.

"Where's Lysandra?" Nicodemus asked. "And does she vouch for this man?"

"I do," Lysandra said as she wriggled out from under the small brass bed where she'd been hiding. She then took great pleasure in freeing her spectacular wings from their cramped state.

"In that case you can stay. We do need the extra help." They finished their introductions and then Nicodemus asked,

"You wouldn't happen to know anything about defeating fairies, would you?"

"Well actually, I do. With mother being so dedicated to their kind I soon learned a lot about them. There are a few easy things we can do that should be just enough to distract them so we can escape." He paused for a moment and then asked, "Where is my mother, by the way?"

"She fled at the first sign of danger. We killed the locusts and Danae but then she escaped on Perseus. We haven't found Zeno yet but I'm hoping he's gone too. I don't mean to be pushy but we must hurry. Ophelia is still out there with all those Dactyls.

They all huddled in close together and Diomede began; "Firstly we should turn all our clothes inside out; this confuses the fairies and will give us a head start." Cleopatra and Thaddea went behind the screen while Nicodemus and Diomede swapped their clothes around. "Secondly, does anyone have any bread or oatmeal?"

"Yes," said Nicodemus. He pulled some crusty bread from his saddlebag and handed it to Diomede who began breaking it into pieces.

"Right," he said, "everyone is to put some of this in their pockets as protection. Fairies don't like to approach if you have some. What about any Christian symbols?"

"No, sorry." Everyone shook their heads.

"You carry on," Cleopatra said. "I'll have a look around."

"Um, what else? Come on, man, think! I know there were loads of things—I just can't think. That's it! Bells! They hate bells! They'll run away."

"I don't happen to carry bells around with me, I'm afraid. I'm not an English Morris dancer you know." Nicodemus' anxieties were clearly getting the better of him.

"Father, that's enough," Thaddea said. "He's only trying to help and I do have some bells in my rucksack. Elora and I had been using them to practise for the Festival of the Crops." Thaddea was just a little bit perturbed at her father's behaviour. She offered Diomede the bells but he insisted she keep them for her safety.

"Here, look what I've found," Cleopatra said as she joined the others. "It's mothers crucifix. Father must had hidden it in here when she died."

"Great," Diomede said. "Now you must wear it and it will keep you safe. I shall go out first and take this mirror with me." He took a small face mirror off the dressing table. "And you are all to follow me making as much noise as possible. Thaddea, you shake those bells like your life depended on it."

"It does," she said

"Right. Well, get shaking then; and we need to keep Balthasa and Delia in the middle because they don't have any protection. Everyone ready? Okay let's go." He pushed open the door and they came bursting out shouting, waving arms, bells and crosses and generally causing total confusion to the Dactyls who had been lying in wait.

In seconds it was all over. Their plan had worked perfectly: the Dactyls couldn't cope and one by one disappeared for good. They couldn't celebrate yet, though, for there was still Ophelia to think of. They stampeded along the corridor and down the stairs to where she lay.

"Phe, wake up! Come on! Don't die on me now we've made it. Come on, Phe, please!" Nicodemus was crouched down and shaking her in anguish. Then he stopped, stood up, wagged his finger crossly and said, "Now listen to me, you old trout, you told me you were immortal, so quit mucking around and wake up." Then he shoved his hands on his hips like one with great authority would do.

"And you told me you weren't sure you were a 'conqueror for the people'! Well, you great lump, I think you are and it's about time you did too!" Ophelia rose steadily to her feet and gave a tentative shake to make her bristles stand to attention. Then she added: "And if you ever call me old trout again I'll refuse to fly you anywhere!" And she finished with an infectious giggle.

Nicodemus was so exhilarated he grabbed Thaddea under the arms and swung her round until he was dizzy. (Must be a man thing, Cleopatra thought.) "There's just one thing left to do then," he said.

"What's that?" Diomede asked.

"Find the Beryl Stone and go home."

"That's two!" Ophelia said, evidently happy to be back in the land of the living.

"Watch you don't cut yourself on your sharp wit, Phe. Now come here so I can give you a big hug and finish what we came here to do."

"Right you are, sir."

"When you two have quite finished," Balthasa interrupted the foolhardiness, "I know where your stone is, so once again, let's go."

They landed in a pretty courtyard that had a beautifully crafted water feature, which sat majestically as a centrepiece upon an awe-inspiring mosaic floor. To the right of it was the love seat that Stefan and Hestia used to relax on while they listened to the gentle ripples of the water. And to the left, joy of joys, was the Beryl Stone in all its glory. Nicodemus walked over to it and respectfully ran his hands across the sparkling Aquamarine. "Come on, let's take you home," he whispered and brought his hand to rest on the glittering silver band. As he looked down he could see a mysterious shadow moving through the patterns in the floor. He slowly raised his head to see the shadow purposefully striding away from him. Zeno, he thought fleetingly. Then he brought his attention back to the stone. "Balthasa, would you do me the honour of carrying this around your neck and taking it back to the sacred palm for me?"

"It would be a privilege." So Nicodemus carefully slipped the ring over Balthasa's head and said.

"So everybody, for one last time…"

"LET'S GO!" they all said in harmony.

They arrived back at the sacred palm very quickly. (Journeys always seem to be faster on the way home—I don't know if you find that?) They were delighted at all being reunited. Ximena's head wound was healing fast and Aldara's wings were on the mend, although she would never fly at top speed again. Cadmus had cleared his lungs of smoke and was in good spirits. Tyrone was still unable to fly due to the crack in his shell, so they set to work weaving a hammock made from threads taken from the trunk of the sacred palm. Then they attached rope to the four corners and ran one under the middle and up either side, giving six points for carrying.

Gently they helped Tyrone into the centre, and then the friends gallantly took off—Diomede on Ulysses and Cleopatra on Lysandra pulling from the front. The immensely strong Balthasa supported the middle from one side, with Stefan, Larissa and Ximena on board, helped by Thaddea and Delia on the other side. Bringing up the rear were Cadmus, Aldara and Ophelia, not forgetting Nicodemus, an unlikely hero some people may think, but despite his appearance—he was in fact, Nicodemus—'Conqueror for the People'.

ENDS

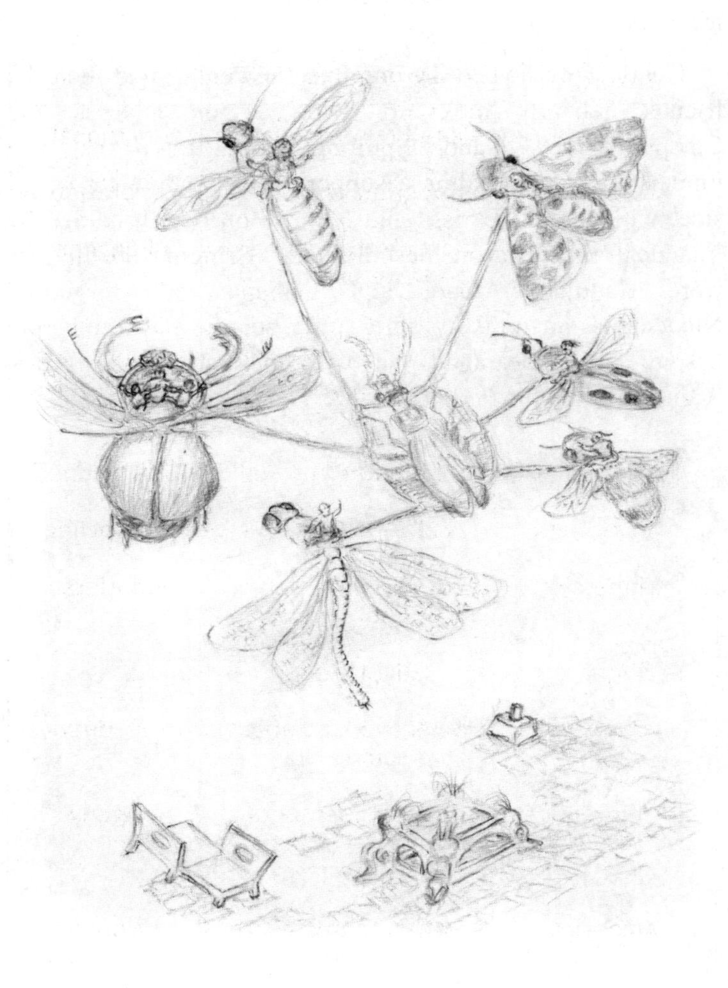

"LET'S GO!" they all said in harmony.

Glossary

Word	Meaning	Alternative
Absurd	Totally unreasonable	Irrational
Abundance	A great amount	Profusion
Acrid	Nasty bitter or sharp taste or smell	Pungent
Adrenaline	A chemical reaction in the body to make it work harder and faster	-
Aerodynamic	Designed to fly well	Streamlined
Agonising	Extremely painful	Harrowing
Aimlessly	With no direction or purpose	Pointlessly
Ajar	Slightly open	-
Angst	Being worried about something	Anxiety
Anguish	Severe mental or physical pain or suffering	Agony
Anxieties	Things that concern you	Worries
Apprehensive	Worried about what might happen	Anxious
Atrocities	Extremely cruel	Inhumanities

	actions	
Audacity	Boldness in a rude way	Defiance
Austere	Severe or strict in appearance and manner	Stern
Assassination	Kill someone	Murder
Avail	To benefit from	Help
Avenge	Get your own back	Retaliate
Awash	Overflowing with something	Inundated
Awe inspiring	Giving someone a feeling of great respect, admiration and wonder	Breathtaking
Barrage	Constant supply of words or questions	Bombardment
Barren	Lacking in vegetation	Wasteland
Bedraggled	Untidy, dirty, messy	Unkempt
Begrudgingly	To allow unwillingly	Reluctantly
Bellowed	To shout in a deep voice	Hollered
Bemused	To be confused	Bewildered
Beseech	To beg for earnestly	Implore
Betray	Be disloyal to someone	Deceived

Bewilderment	State of confusion	Bafflement
Blearily	Exhausted, worn out	Tiredly
Broach	Raise a subject for discussion	Mention
Buckled	Gave way under pressure	Crumpled
Brutally	In a vicious manner	Savagely
Celadon	Very pale green	-
Ceremoniously	Done in a formal and grand way	Resplendently
Charade	Silly pretending	Pretence
Chasm	A deep hole in the ground	Gorge
Claustrophobic	Uncomfortably closed in	Confined
Colony	A group of animals/insects living together	Settlement
Commotion	A loud outburst	Disturbance
Compos mentis	Having full control of your mind	Of sound mind
Conceded	Admitted that something was true	Accepted
Congealed	Become semi solid	Coagulated
Concocting	Making something up	Inventing

Consciousness	Being aware of yourself and your situation	Awareness
Consecutive	Following one after another	Successive
Constricting	Closing tightly	Narrowing
Contemplate	Think about something	Ponder
Conveyed	Passed on information	Communicated
Convoy	A group travelling together	Procession
Corroboration	Give support to something	Confirmation
Culprit	Person responsible for doing something wrong	Perpetrator
Crevices	Narrow openings or cracks in rocks or walls	Fissures
Debilitated	Severely weakened	Enervated
Debris	Pieces of something destroyed	Rubble
Decipher	Work out something that's confusing	Interpret
Defiance	Strength and boldness to challenge	Resistance

Definitive	A final decision	Conclusive
Demeanour	The way a person behaves	Manner
Derelict	In a very poor condition	Ramshackle
Desecrating	Treat something special with disrespect	Violating
Desolation	Something has been ruined	Devastation
Despairingly	Acting without hope	Hopelessly
Despondent	Very sad without much hope	Disheartened
Deter	Try to stop someone doing something	Discourage
Devour	Eat up greedily	Gobble
Dilapidated	In poor condition, due to neglect	Run down
Dilemma	A difficult situation that has no easy solution	Quandary
Diminished	Became less	Decrease
Diplomacy	Handle a situation considerately	Finesse
Discharged	Removed from duties	Dismissed
Disembarked	Get off a ship, plane	Debark

	or train	
Dishevelled	Untidy in appearance	Unkempt
Divulge	Tell something that was secret	Disclose
Dulcet	Sweet and soothing	Pleasant
Dumbfounded	Speechless with amazement	Flabbergasted
Ecstatic	Feeling great delight	Elated
Empowered	To gain strength from an action taken	Liberated
Endearing	Inspiring love or affection	Adorable
Endured	Put up with	Tolerated
Engulf	Swallow up or overwhelm	Immerse
Entwined	Twisted together	Enlaced
Envied	Wanted something someone else had	Be jealous of
Epitome	A typical example	Model
Errand	A short trip to deliver and collect something	Task
Evidently	In an obvious manner	Clearly
Exasperated	Being really irritated or annoyed	Infuriated

Excruciating	Unbearably painful	Agonising
Exhilarated	Feeling happy and full of energy	Elated
Exposed	Without shelter, out in the open	Unprotected
Exquisite	Extremely attractive	Beautiful
Extent	The size or scale of something	Length
Extinguishing	Putting out a fire	Dousing
Façade	Misleading appearance	Charade
Fate	Final outcome	Destiny
Ferociously	Extremely savage	Fiercely
Feverishly	Intense activity	Frantically
Finery	Smart clothes or decoration	Regalia
Formidable	Unnervingly powerful and impressive	Intimidating
Fortuitous	Happening by chance	Lucky
Frenzy	Wild and uncontrollable behaviour	Hysteria
Gallantly	Acting in a brave and heroic way	Valiantly

Gloat	To show off about your own success	Boast
Harrumphed	A throaty sound expressing disapproval	-
Haste	Hurry or rush an action	Speed
Heightened	Became more extreme	Increased
Ignorant	Lacking knowledge	Unaware
Imbecile	A stupid or silly person	Cretin
Imminent	About to occur	Forthcoming
Immortal	Does not die	Eternal
Impending	About to happen	Imminent
Imperative	Very important	Vital
Implicitly	Without doubt or question	Completely
Implore	To beg for urgently	Plead
Impressionable	Easily influenced	Suggestible
Improvised	To make up on the spot	Extemporized
Impulsively	Without thinking	Impetuously
Incensed	To be extremely angry	Outraged

Inconspicuously	Without being noticed	Unobtrusively
Incorrigible	Impossible to control or manage	Intractable
Incubator	A heated enclosed box to hatch chicks	Brooder
Indispensable	Absolutely necessary	Essential
Inferno	Large uncontrollable fire	Conflagration
Inflicted	Did something in an unpleasant manner	Forced
Influx	A mass arrival	Inundation
Inhabitant	A person or animal who lives in a particular place	Resident
Initially	At the beginning	Primarily
Insipid	Lacking in colour and character	Jejune
Insolence	Being rude	Impertinence
Intensity	Extreme degrees of something	Harshness
Intermittent	Stopping and starting	Periodic
Intimidating	Filling you with fear	Frightening
Intoxicating	Causing you to lose control	Inebriating

Invincible	Incapable of being defeated	Unbeatable
Irony	Different to what is expected	Absurdity
Jeopardy	A source of danger	At Risk
Lethargy	Lack of energy	Sluggishness
Majestically	Impressively grand or beautiful	Stately
Manifest	Show or display	Reveal
Manoeuvre	A movement requiring skill and care	Operation
Melancholy	Sad and depressed	Gloomy
Menacing	A threatening quality	Forbidding
Mesmerised	Have your attention fixed on something	Fascinated
Migrating	Moving to warm places in winter and cool ones in summer	Relocating
Mortar	Mixture of cement, lime sand and water that ticks bricks together	-
Mortified	To feel uncomfortable because of shame	Embarrassed

Mournfully	Showing sadness	Sorrowfully
Naivety	Lack of experience or wisdom	Innocence
Nifty	A quick skilful action	Agile
Oaf	Stupid, rude and clumsy man	Lout
Oblivious	Not knowing what is going on around you	Unaware
Ominous	Giving the impression something bad is going to happen	Baleful
Optimist	A person who is hopeful and confident about the future/outcome	-
Ordeal	A long and awful experience	Hardship
Pandemonium	A scene of confusion	Bedlam
Paparazzi	People who take photographs of celebrities	-
Pendulum	A swinging weight used to regulate a clock	-
Perturbed	Made anxious or unsettled	Upset
Phenomenal	Exceedingly good	Outstanding
Plummeting	Falling straight down	Nose diving

	at high speed	
Pompous	Having a high opinion of yourself	Pontifical
Pondered	Considered something carefully	Contemplated
Precariously	Dangerously lacking in safety	Perilously
Precautionary	Action taken to avoid danger	Preventative
Precision	The quality of doing something exactly	Accuracy
Predator	An animal that kills other animals	-
Predecessor	Someone who had the job before you	Forerunner
Predicament	A difficult situation to be in	Dilemma
Premise	A result based on something thought to be true	Assumption
Preoccupied	Concerned about something	Distracted
Profusely	In large amounts	Copious
Propelled	Moved forward with force	Launched
Proposition	Situation to be dealt with	Undertaking

Protruded	Stuck out	Jutted
Prudently	To act carefully in your own interest	Cautiously
Psychopathic	Mentally ill	Insane
Pulsating	Expanding and contracting like a heartbeat	Throbbing
Quest	Searching for something	Pursuit
Rabid	Infected with rabies	-
Radiance	Shine brightly	Brilliance
Rasping	Unpleasant harsh sound	Grating
Ravine	A deep narrow steep sided valley	Gorge
Realisation	Become fully aware of something	Comprehension
Recuperate	Recover from illness or tiredness	Convalesce
Refuge	A place providing shelter	Safety
Rejuvenate	Rest and get more energy	Restore
Relapse	Become ill again after having felt better	Deterioration
Remnants	Something that remains	Leftovers

Rendering	Causing something to become something else	Making
Rendezvous	A prearranged place to get together	Meeting
Reprimanded	Tell someone off angrily	Chastised
Reprobates	Bad people	Villains
Resolve	Decision on action to be taken	Undertaking
Retaliated	Got your own back for a wrong doing	Reciprocated
Reunited	Bring 2 or more people together again	Together again
Revelation	Something surprising	Confession
Reverberating	Repeating as an echo	Resounding
Rigorously	Extremely thoroughly	Meticulously
Sauntered	Walk in a slow relaxed manner	Strolled
Scoffed	Speaking to someone as if they are useless	Jeered
Scrutinizing	Examining thoroughly	Inspecting
Secluded	Private and sheltered	Hidden
Shimmy	Shake and wiggle your body	Wriggle

Shuddered	To shiver uncomfortably	Quivered
Silhouette	The outline of a dark shape against a light background	Profile
Sincere	Not pretending or deceiving	Genuine
Sinister	Threatening or suggesting evil	Menacing
Sombre	Serious, sad or gloomy	Melancholy
Soporific	Causing drowsiness or sleep	Somnolent
Stark	Complete	Total
Submissive	Quietly obedient	Meek
Subsided	Became less strong	Abated
Subtly	A slight change making it hard to notice	Understated
Succumb	To give in reluctantly	Yield
Summoned	Ordered someone to come	Sent for
Surmised	To guess as don't have enough evidence	Speculated
Sustaining	Experiencing something awful	Suffering
Sustenance	Things to feed the	Nourishment

	body	
Sweltering	Uncomfortably hot	Stilfling
Tannoy	Loud speaker system	Loudspeaker
Tarpaulin	Sheet of heavy waterproof cloth	-
Tentatively	In an uncertain way	Hesitantly
Terrain	An area of land with specific features	Topography
Torrential	Falling rapidly and heavily	Teeming
Tranquillity	State of calmness	Stillness
Trepidation	Feeling nervous about something	Apprehension
Trivia	Something that is not very important	Trifle
Turmoil	Extreme confusion	Upheaval
Unbeknownst	Without someone's knowledge	-
Unscathed	Not injured	Unharmed
Unwavering	Remaining strong, never weakening	Unfaltering
Unyielding	Remaining firm and determined	Tenacious
Vibrant	Full of energy	Vivacious
Vigilantly	Looking out for	Watchfully

	things, being on alert	
Vigorously	With great strength and energy	Strenuously
Vouch	Confirm someone is who they say they are	Confirm
Vulnerable	Likely to be physically or emotionally hurt	Exposed
Waning	Gradually decreasing	Dwindling
Wretched	A behaviour that you don't like	Vile
Writhed	To twist in pain	Contorted
Yearned	To have a strong desire to do something	Hankered